Richard reached out and grasped Liana's face between the long fingers of his hands. "This face," he muttered. "This damnably beautiful face."

"No," she answered, her fragile shield of composure shattering with his touch, and in its place a treacherous need sprang to life.

"Yes, its beauty is indelibly burned on the brain of every man who's ever seen it," he said, stepping closer, his body brushing against hers, making her nerves come alive with pleasure and pain.

"You're exaggerating. My lips are too big," she said desperately.

"They're full and sensuous and make a man fantasize about sealing his lips to them for a month at a time."

"You're wrong," she said softly, then tried again. "My eyebrows feather instead of going in a straight line."

"They make a man wonder if there's something not quite tame beneath that perfect control you project."

Liana struggled to draw air into her lungs, but the air seared her like a desert wind. Richard began to brush her jaw with his fingers, touching her gently, then intensifying the pressure.

"Your face," he whispered fiercely. "Your mouth, your eyes, your skin, your damned sexy body."

"Richard . . ." The ruthlessness of his expression frightened her, excited her.

"It's all right," he muttered. "I'm immune." And then he brought his mouth down hard on hers, and she knew she could never escape him. . . .

WHAT ARE *LOVESWEPT* ROMANCES?

They are stories of true romance and touching emotion. We believe those two very important ingredients are constants in our highly sensual and very believable stories in the *LOVESWEPT* line. Our goal is to give you, the reader, stories of consistently high quality that may sometimes make you laugh, sometimes make you cry, but are always fresh and creative and contain many delightful surprises within their pages.

Most romance fans read an enormous number of books. Those they truly love, they keep. Others may be traded with friends and soon forgotten. We hope that each *LOVESWEPT* romance will be a treasure—a "keeper." We will always try to publish

LOVE STORIES YOU'LL NEVER FORGET
BY AUTHORS YOU'LL ALWAYS REMEMBER

The Editors

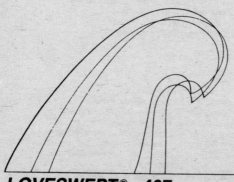

LOVESWEPT® • 407

Fayrene Preston
SwanSea Place:
Deceit

 BANTAM BOOKS
NEW YORK • TORONTO • LONDON • SYDNEY • AUCKLAND

DECEIT

A Bantam Book / May 1990

LOVESWEPT® *and the wave device are registered*
trademarks of Bantam Books, a division of
Bantam Doubleday Dell Publishing Group, Inc.
Registered in U.S. Patent
and Trademark Office and elsewhere.

If you would be interested in receiving protective vinyl
covers for your Loveswept books, please write to this address
for information:

Loveswept
Bantam Books
P.O. Box 985
Hicksville, NY 11802

ISBN 0-553-44017-9

Published simultaneously in the United States and Canada

Bantam Books are published by Bantam Books, a division
of Bantam Doubleday Dell Publishing Group, Inc. Its trade-
mark, consisting of the words "Bantam Books" and the
portrayal of a rooster, is Registered in U.S. Patent and
Trademark Office and in other countries. Marca Registrada.
Bantam Books, 666 Fifth Avenue, New York, New York 10103.

PRINTED IN THE UNITED STATES OF AMERICA

OPM   0 9 8 7 6 5 4 3 2 1

Preface

Lights glimmered in every window of SwanSea. Inside, dance music reverberated through the elegant rooms and hallways. And in the ballroom exquisitely dressed couples whirled gaily, the women's jewels flashing like fire.

A quarter of a mile away, on a lonely windswept cliff, Leonora Deverell could hear the strains of the waltz as she paced in the iron gazebo.

Where was he?

Pausing a moment, she glanced up at the big yellow moon that hung over SwanSea and tried to judge the time. At least an hour had passed since the grandfather clock in the foyer had struck midnight. Anxiously she clasped her hands together. The carriage was waiting for them, their bags already in it. John's nurse had packed all of his clothes and toys, and if she were following the schedule, had probably already tucked him comfortably into the carriage. It would be a long, tiring journey for the three year old, and Leonora hoped he would sleep all the way to Boston where they would board the ship for Europe.

Where was he?

Be calm, she told herself. Everything was going to be fine. For the first time in her life she had discovered love. She was happy and full of anticipation for the future.

Suddenly she heard footsteps and eagerly turned. But at the sight of her husband standing before her, she went cold all over.

"Leonora, it is time for you to come back to the ball now. It is almost over and you will want to bid our guests goodnight."

Their only illumination was moonlight, but she had no trouble making out the glittering anger in his cobalt blue eyes. "Edward, I—"

"You will have to change back into your ball gown, of course. I am not sure our guests would understand if you were wearing a traveling suit."

He was so tall, so big, so hard. In the four years they had been married, she had never crossed him, but her love for Wyatt had given her a courage she had never known before. "I cannot live with you any longer, Edward. I have tried to make our marriage work, but you care nothing for me. There is no love between us, and I feel as if I am withering from the lack of it." She paused. "Edward, I am leaving you."

"No, Leonora, you are not." He thrust out his hand toward her, the gesture an order. "Come with me. Your maid is waiting to help you change. If we're quick enough, no one need ever know about this."

"That's all you care about, isn't it?" she asked, despair making her voice quiver. "Appearances. Gaining acceptance into society."

"I don't have time to discuss this with you."

"You *never* have time to discuss *anything* with

me, Edward. I thought all men were like that until I met Wyatt."

His teeth came together with a snap. "Wyatt Redmond is an impoverished painter I *hired* to paint your portrait. Surely you wouldn't make a fool out of yourself over a nobody like him."

"He isn't a nobody," she said, tears clogging her throat. "He is the man I love."

"He can offer you nothing."

"He can offer me everything that matters."

For a brief moment, a look of genuine bewilderment crossed his face. "I don't understand. I have given you everything you desired. The grandest house in America. Beautiful clothes. Why, the gown you wore tonight was designed by Worth of Paris, and you have one of the finest collections of jewelry in the country." His finger flicked the topaz, ivory, and gold lily she wore on her lapel.

She stiffened, afraid for a moment he would realize the lily was not among the many pieces of jewelry he had given her. Then she realized it no longer mattered.

"Those were the things *you* desired, Edward. They were possessions for your possession. I wanted only your love."

"Love?" His tone indicated he thought her insane.

"I am leaving, Edward, and you cannot stop me."

His hand snaked out and closed on her wrist. "You will not take my son."

She had feared discovery for this very reason. Edward was obsessed with having children, and John was the only child she had been able to give him. She swallowed. "Of course John will go with me. I am his mother."

"What kind of mother would want to take her son from his father? What kind of mother would expose her son to the adulterous relationship she has with her lover? I tell you, I will not have it. I absolutely will not allow the scandal. No, Leonora. John stays with me." Edward leaned closer and closer still. His face almost touching hers, he cruelly tightened his hold on her wrist, bruising her soft flesh. "Think about this very carefully, Leonora. Because the only way you will leave me is if you are dead."

She stared at him, stricken.

And neither of them noticed that behind them, the lights of SwanSea were going out, one by one.

One

He positioned himself unobtrusively among the onlookers of the photographic shoot and fixed his steel gray gaze on the world-famous model, Liana Marchall. She was the epitome of serenity and beauty as she stood at the top of the marble stairs beneath the tall, stained glass Tiffany window that suggested the living form of a peacock's head and body.

The peacock motif continued in a mosaic representing the vivid plumage of the tail. It trailed down the grand stairway and onto the floor of the great hall where he stood. It was breathtaking, but it was nothing in comparison to the woman, he reflected, using utter objectivity.

She was a living work of art. She lacked only two things to make her perfect: a heart and a soul.

His fingers idly rubbed the white-on-white *RZ* monogram on his shirt's cuff while he studied the people with whom she was working. Through inquiries, he had learned that the photographer, Clay Phillips, was relatively unknown and was here only because the great Jean-Paul Savion, one of the top fashion photographers in the business, had come down with a virus on his last trip to the Middle East and had been forced to remain at his home in Paris.

His mouth quirked. *What a shame.*

"How's it going, Rosalyn?" he heard Clay call up to the middle-aged woman who had been brushing extra color onto Liana's perfect cheekbones. "Are you finished?"

Stroking her skin had been like stroking the inside of a flower petal. His fingers flexed, and he slipped his hands into the pockets of his tailor-made gray slacks.

Rosalyn stepped back and critically eyed Liana's face, then reached up and combed a shining strand of wheat-colored hair into place. "Yes," she said finally and somewhat disappointedly, "I'm finished."

"Great," Clay said. The corner of his mouth twitched slightly, and he rubbed the area immediately below his belt.

The man's stomach had to be in knots, he thought. Before this, Clay Phillips had only worked under Savion. He had to view this opportunity as a huge, almost miraculous break.

"Steve, bring the key light down two stops and move that wind machine exactly three inches to the right and set it on low. Got it?"

"Got it," the younger man named Steve said laconically. He wore a pair of bleached-out blue jeans, a nondescript T-shirt, and his hair long and slightly curly.

He was good at his job, he thought, observing him, *but he didn't look prosperous enough to be Liana's type.* The photographer could be another story, though. Maybe Liana had decided her star would be lifted even higher if she helped another photographer achieve fame.

Suddenly Clay lifted his head and swept his gaze around the great hall as if he were searching the air. "What in the hell is that awful music?"

"Gershwin," Steve said, then grinned. "George Gershwin."

"Gershwin? Where's *our* music? U2? The Rolling Stones? The Beatles? Sara, did you check into this?"

Clay's abrupt question was directed at the young woman who knelt beside him, loading film into one of his many cameras. She flipped a long, sleek swag of red hair behind her shoulder. "The management said positively no rock music," she said quietly.

Clay frowned. "What decade are these people living in?"

"I asked something like that and was told that this is SwanSea."

"What does that mean?"

"Offhand I'd say it means no rock music," Steve said dryly, sending a wink in Sara's direction. She smiled shyly back.

"Oh," Clay said, his tone and gaze indicating his mind was already on something else, namely his model.

Who could blame him, he wondered cynically.

Clay gestured to Sara and pointed at the camera he wanted her to hand him. "Good, then let's go to work. Liana, darling, are you ready?"

"Yes," Liana said, relieved that the waiting was over.

Oblivious to the frenzy of activity at the base of the staircase, Liana clasped the silk chiffon skirt of her strapless haute-couture gown between her fingertips. With each movement, the dress appeared to change color, one moment a teal blue, the next, a shimmering green. Rather than seeing an actual color, a person received an impression of the two colors that was much like the iridescent eye of a peacock feather. The fabric had been specially woven to produce this effect and was a compliment to the Tiffany window, the marble mosaic of the staircase, and Liana's famous teal-colored eyes.

The first straining notes of "Rhapsody in Blue" began to rise. With the material still clasped in her hands, she spread her arms in a V above and behind her head and started her descent, crossing back and forth across the staircase.

As she glided downward, the blue-green silk chiffon fluttered like wings, making her appear as if she were some exotic bird about to take flight.

Below her, Clay scrambled to take shot after shot. "Beautiful, wonderful. Can you raise your arms more? Now lower them. Look down. Good. Over your shoulder—"

Liana, lost in the image she and Clay were creating, followed his instructions to the letter. She'd done it a thousand times. These were her favorite moments, when she could forget Liana, the woman, and focus on Liana, the model, and how best she could sell whatever product her face and her body were showcasing. In this instance, it was the idea of elegance and glamour that would be produced by the combination of her, the dress, and SwanSea.

All at once, a light crashed to the floor, jerking her from her state of concentration. Electricity flashed and hot glass flew outward. With one high-heeled shoe poised midair for the next step, Liana hesitated, glancing to see what had happened.

Her gaze collided with a pair of steel gray eyes, and for a moment everything stood still. As her lips formed the name, *Richard*, darkness rushed in to circle her, she lost her balance, her heel twisted, and she began to fall.

Her knee struck the marble, pain shot through her. There would be more pain to come, she thought vaguely, and held out her hands in an attempt to protect herself. Then hard arms caught her against a solidly muscled chest, a masculine scent of musk and spices enveloped her, and she knew that though she was no longer in danger from harming herself on the marble staircase, she would not be as lucky with Richard Zagen.

"You might as well open those beautiful eyes, Liana, because I'm not going away. Not this minute, at any rate."

She didn't remember his voice having such a sharp, cutting edge, she thought hazily. But then again, maybe, on that last day in Paris, it had. She braced herself as if she were about to smash into a brick wall going a hundred miles an hour and did as he said.

The years had given his face a hard, cynical cast. His dark brown hair appeared as crisp and vital as ever, but the silver at the temples was new, and the muscles she could feel in his arms and chest suggested an even greater strength than before. All in all, he was still the most attractive man she had ever known.

Her gaze touched on the sardonic curl of his lips, then returned to the steel gray eyes. "Hello, Richard."

"So you do remember me? I wasn't sure. I thought perhaps you'd had so many victims in the past eleven years that the first one might have slipped your mind."

"Are you hurt, Liana?" Clay asked, stooped down beside them and taking her hand. "I nearly had a heart attack, watching you fall."

Sara, Rosalyn, and Steve stood anxiously in a circle around them.

"Lord, Liana, I'm sorry," Steve said. "I got caught up in watching you and I guess I leaned against the light. I should have known better."

"It's all right." She pushed away from Richard and sat up. "I'm okay." Her voice was shaking. Though she wasn't surprised, she tried to rectify the matter with her next words. "My knee hurts a little, but I'm fine." Good, she thought. She sounded stronger.

Richard jerked the long skirt up to look at her knee. It was bruised and bloodied.

Liana groaned with dismay. "Oh, no, the dress has blood on it."

"To hell with the dress," Richard muttered, gently feeling the area around the open wound. "What about broken bones?"

"He's right, darling," Clay said and missed the sharp look Richard shot him at the word *darling*. "Can you extend your leg?"

"I think so." Trying not to grimace, she stretched the leg outward.

"Does that hurt?" Clay asked.

"Not too bad."

Richard had been watching her closely. "You may not have any broken bones, but the human body wasn't made for bouncing off marble. You need to see a doctor."

"No, really—"

Clay looked up at Sara. "Check and see if they can get a doctor out here quickly."

"Clay, really, it's nothing."

"When the doctor tells me that, I'll believe you." He pressed her arm with his hand. "You're very valuable to us, Liana."

Abruptly, Richard scooped her into his arms and stood. "I'll take you up to your room."

"No!" The jolt of her fall and the initial shock of

seeing Richard had worn off. Now she had to deal with the hard, cold fact that Richard was actually here at SwanSea. Not only that, he was holding her, and all her senses were clamoring as if it were eleven years ago and she and Richard were back in Paris. It would never do. She couldn't allow the situation to continue. She'd heard the alarm contained in her outburst. Fortunately, over the years she'd learned to adopt a mood at the drop of a hat, and now she wrapped herself in calm as easily as if it were a designer gown. "Please put me down, Richard. I can walk."

He tightened his arms around her and started down the stairs. "You can prove that after the doctor looks at you. Until then, you should stay off the knee."

Surprise at Richard's proprietary manner with Liana held Clay still for a moment, but he caught his breath quickly and said, "Wait a minute. Do you know this man, Liana?"

She looked at Clay without seeing him. It was taking every ounce of her energy to retain her calm demeanor and to fight the steadily growing panic inside her. The warmth and strength of Richard's body was sapping her will. Instinct was telling her to slide her arms around his neck and melt against him. Logic and reason were telling her that would be an exceedingly dangerous thing for her to do.

"Liana?" Clay asked.

Richard gazed down at her. "Yes, Liana. I'm waiting to hear what you're going to say, too. I'm sure you'll use *old* as a modifier, but I can't even guess what noun you'll choose."

Clay planted his fists at his sides. "What's he talking about?"

"Richard is an old . . . acquaintance."

Richard laughed flatly. "The easy way out. I suppose I should have known."

His hard, sarcastic tone was beginning to hurt more than her knee. "Dammit, Richard, put me down."

"So you've learned to curse. I'm overcome with admiration, not to mention curiosity. What else have you learned?"

"Richard—"

"For instance, have you learned any really hot lovemaking tricks? Now that would really impress me."

She darted an embarrassed glance at Clay as warmth flared in her cheeks.

"Are you ready to let me take you up to your room without protest now?"

She noted his satisfied expression with a flash of anger. "You embarrassed me on purpose."

"I do everything on purpose these days, Liana. Now be a good girl and tell your photographer that I'm not abducting you against your will. Or would you like me to embarrass you some more?"

She briefly closed her eyes. "It's all right, Clay. I'll be more comfortable in my room. Just send the doctor up when he comes."

"Very good," Richard said with mocking approval. "Now what room are you in?"

"Thirty-three."

"How convenient. I'm just down the hall."

Liana had immediately fallen in love with her room at SwanSea. Light and airy, it overlooked a wide green lawn and the endless sea beyond and had been decorated in harmonious colors and soft textures. Even the strong shapes of the light-toned furniture were softened by inlays and floral decorations.

The bed's four tall posters rose in graceful swirls of carved satinwood. Swags of sea foam green chiffon looped from the top of one poster to the next, then spilled down to the floor to form diaphanous pools.

Until now Liana had felt the mood of the room was soothing. But that was before Richard had invaded its space.

He carefully settled her on the couch, then stood back and eyed her critically. "Raise your skirt."

She started. "I beg your pardon."

His lips twisted. "Don't flatter yourself, Liana. If I wanted to take you to bed, I would. For now, I just want you to lift your skirt off your knee so that the material won't become stuck to the wound."

She didn't trust him or his motives and knew he should be treated with the utmost caution, but his constant taunting had stretched her nerves to the limit. "Look, Richard," she began, the cadence of her words deliberately slow to ensure the steadiness of her voice, "you saved me from falling down the stairs. You've carried me up here. I'm grateful."

"Be still my heart. Liana Marchall is grateful to me."

Her teeth ground together. "*But* I'd appreciate it if you would leave now. I'll be fine until the doctor arrives."

He leaned down to look her in the eye. "You're close to the top of the list of the ten most desirable women in the world, Liana. That's a unique power all its own. But you'll never have enough power to dismiss me. Not again."

"I didn't mean—"

"Oh, yes, sweetheart, you did mean. You were trying to get rid of me, but this time, it won't work—not unless I'm ready to leave." He straightened, spun on his heels, and headed for the bathroom.

Liana pressed her hand to her heart to restrain its wild beating. It was a vain attempt. *This had to be another of her sweet, unbearable nightmares.* Her dreams of Richard over the years had sometimes been so real that, when she woke, she would roll over, absolutely sure that she would find him beside her. Always there would be nothing but an empty pillow.

But now he was here; she was undoubtedly wide awake; and her memories and dreams were nothing in comparison to the vital, entirely compelling, masculine reality of him.

He returned to the room with a wet washcloth, knelt in front of her, and cupped his left hand behind her knee. With a light delicate touch so at odds with such a tough man, he sponged the blood away from the broken skin. "This isn't too bad," he murmured.

She stared down at his bent head. She wasn't surprised to find his hair still thick and glossy, but she was surprised that her fingers tingled to touch it. "What are you doing here at SwanSea, Richard?"

His steel gray gaze sliced up to her, cold and impenetrable.

Her throat moved convulsively. "I just wondered. I mean, you're a very important man. Your company has grown twenty times bigger since . . ." Her voice trailed off.

"You've kept track of me?"

"It's not hard to do. Over the years, I've occasionally picked up the business section of the newspaper. Sometimes there'd be an article about you."

And then there'd been that time, six years ago, right after her father's death when she'd attempted to see him. She'd gone straight from the funeral to the airport and booked herself on the next flight to New York. Immediately upon landing in New York, she'd called his office, only to be told by his secretary that he was on his honeymoon.

"Save yourself some anguish, Liana. You have nothing to do with my being here."

"I didn't think—"

His knowing smile made the words abruptly die in her throat. That was *exactly* what she had thought.

"I came because of the auction of art nouveau works that will be held in a few days."

"Are you a collector?"

He nodded. "And there are quite a few noteworthy paintings up for sale." His gruff, harsh tone was startling in its contrast to the incredibly gentle way he ministered to her knee. "And I'll save you the effort of asking the next question. Yes, I knew you were going to be here."

Her muscles tightened with alarm; her words rushed out in a whisper. "Then, why?"

"I didn't find out about the fact that you would be here until after I'd booked my reservations. But I decided very quickly it didn't matter, that I'd be damned if I'd let you ruin my first vacation in years and the chance at the paintings." He gave her knee a final pat with the cloth, then surged to his feet. "Besides, Liana, it's a small world. We were bound to run into each other sooner or later."

She wondered what he'd say if he knew the lengths to which she'd gone to make sure they didn't end up in the same place at the same time. "You're right. It doesn't matter. Besides, SwanSea is a large resort. I'm sure we're both going to be busy with different agendas."

She was no more at a disadvantage with him looming above her than she had been when he'd been kneeling in front of her, but she was relieved when he disappeared into the bathroom to return the washcloth. His absence was a chance for her pulse to return to normal. Unfortunately as soon as he walked back into the room, it began to race again.

His smile, a slash of white teeth, told her he knew how he affected her. "Are you here at SwanSea alone?"

"No, I'm here with Clay and the others."

"I figured that out, Liana."

"Then—?"

"Are you and Clay lovers?"

He hurled the question at her with such speed and force, it took her a moment to recover from its impact. "He's the photographer in charge of this shoot. I hardly know him."

"Really. Yet he called you darling. What do you call him?"

"Clay."

He smiled. "I remember when you were in awe of photographers. But, of course, back then, they had the power to make you a star, and you wanted to become a star more than anything. Right? Including more than you wanted me."

She absorbed the salvo with hardly a flinch and congratulated herself.

He continued without mercy. "Not that one should exclude the other. Except when one uses the method you chose—going from my bed to Savion's. Damn awkward, Liana." With each word, his voice deteriorated until it was an abrasive rasp. "And of course, there were the things you said. I'm sure you recall, especially the part about you really not loving me at all."

"Clay is the photographer on this assignment," she repeated stonily, "nothing more."

"I see. So you and he aren't lovers unlike you and Savion, who are." His shrug indicated the subject was of supreme indifference to him. "I wondered, that's all, since Clay was very concerned about you, and I didn't see Savion around."

She glanced away. "Jean-Paul is ill. Otherwise he would have been here."

"Oh, I would have bet on that. I'm sure it would take something of catastrophic proportions to keep him away from you."

"If he'd come, his interest would have been only in the assignment." Her teeth snapped together as she emphasized each word. It mattered that he believe her, she realized, and wondered why. After all, it was much too late. "We're all here to work. The opening of SwanSea is a gala event, and this layout will appear worldwide in all the important fashion, society, and news magazines."

"More fame and fortune."

"And more hard work."

"I have no doubt. But then I also have no doubt that you receive a great deal of pleasure from what you do. After all, you and Savion work together most of the time, don't you?"

He was playing a game with her, and she was losing badly. It seemed to her she could feel her nerves fraying, one by one, a condition that absolutely had to be kept from him. If he sensed her weakness where he was concerned, he would close in for the kill. She didn't answer him.

"Tell me something, Liana. I'm curious."

She eyed him warily. "About what?"

"*Have* you learned any hot lovemaking tricks?" He heard her indrawn gasp of breath and went on. "Even when you were a novice you could turn me inside out and make me jump through hoops. What are you like in bed now?"

"It's something you'll never know, Richard."

The smile he gave chilled and transfixed her. So much so, she was unable to move, unable to breathe, unable to stop the painful hammering of her heart against her ribs. When the knock on the door came, she jumped.

One dark brow shot up. "Careful, Liana. That skin of yours is much too pretty to jump out of, especially when it could be put to so many other good uses."

Liana climbed carefully into bed and gratefully sank back against the pillows. Richard had stood silently and observantly by as the doctor had examined her, then applied antibiotic cream and wrapped a large, white gauze bandage around her knee. Thankfully for her peace of mind, he had left with the doctor. After that, visits from Clay, Sara, Rosalyn, and Steve had had to be endured.

Alone at last she found her thoughts only increased her tension and anxiety.

Richard was actually here. They had talked. He had held her. Lord, help her!

When she had known Richard eleven years ago in Paris, he had been a gentle and caring man. Now he was hard, cynical, and cruel. He used razor-edged words, and he made no careless moves.

But if he'd changed, she reflected, so had she.

She was no longer the idealistic, naive young girl she had been at eighteen. At twenty-nine, she was much wiser. She was also so full of pain she couldn't stand to be touched.

She felt as if her skin was too sensitive, and contact with anyone would hurt, violate, or scar her. The idea was all in her mind, of course. She was touched all the time, by hairdressers, makeup artists, designers, and photographers. It was her salvation that she had learned to escape to another place in her mind and block them out.

Suddenly chills of fear shivered through her. She wrapped her arms around her body, but no matter how tightly she hugged herself, she couldn't stop remembering the unexpected encounter with Richard and her reaction to him. The chills worsened.

No real damage had been done, she reassured herself over and over again. But cold fear gripped her, and she knew that if there was another encounter, she might not be able to block him out.

Maybe, if she was lucky, she could avoid him. At any rate, it was something to hope and work for.

But how was she going to deal with the fact that she was responsible for the man he had become?

SwanSea was quiet. Most of the lights in the great house were out. Its guests were resting. Except for one.

Richard leaned back against the doorjamb of the open French doors of his room, his eyes squeezed shut, his jaw tightly clenched. A breeze came off the ocean, fanning him, but it neither cooled him nor dried the sheen of sweat covering his body.

Night sweats. They were brought on by the pain of the past, the uncertainty of the present, and the fear of not knowing how the hell he was going to get through the next day, much less the rest of his life. They often came on him like this when he couldn't sleep and when all he could think of was Liana.

Liana. She had haunted him for eleven years, and in that time he had found that being haunted by her was worse than any ghost. Ghosts were illusory. If you saw one, you might not even be sure of what it was you were looking at.

But Liana. No matter where he went, she was there. As one of the most photographed models in the world, her picture graced countless magazine covers. Every newsstand he passed, every coffee table he sat at, every doctor's waiting room he went into usually held at least one magazine with her picture gracing its cover. Her wide teal eyes would stare out at him, taunting him, reminding him of the one question that drove him to work twenty-hour days.

Success had become the god he worshiped. But nothing was ever enough. There was always one more business triumph to achieve. One more possession to buy.

Yet the emptiness remained. And the question persisted.

Why hadn't she loved him?

Two

Liana rose early and ordered room service, then slowly dressed and ate a leisurely breakfast. Her purpose was to have ample time to compose herself. When she finally left her room, she wanted her nerves well hidden beneath the cool facade of the super model. If she should meet Richard, she wanted no hint of how he affected her to show. It wasn't a perfect plan, she acknowledged, but it was all she could think of for the moment.

At the knock on her bedroom door, Liana's hand jerked, toppling the delicate china cup onto its side and sending hot coffee spilling over the pristine white tablecloth. So much for her plan, she thought with disgust. She hastily righted the cup and snatched up the linen napkin to blot as much as she could of the cup's contents.

When the second knock came, she sighed and threw down the napkin. "Coming."

She used the short walk to the door to prepare herself for whoever might be on the other side. Hopefully, it was Clay or Sara, checking to see if she was ready for today's shoot. Surely it wouldn't be Richard. He hated her. If over the years, she'd had any doubts, their encounter last night had eliminated them.

Still she didn't kid herself. Trying to avoid him would accomplish only so much. Their situation was volatile and unpredictable, and she had to be ready for anything. Half expecting to meet steel gray eyes, she opened the door and was astonished to find a beautiful young woman with cinnamon-colored hair and lovely green-gold eyes.

"Good morning. I'm Caitlin Deverell-DiFrenza. I hope I'm not disturbing you."

Liana recognized the name immediately. Caitlin Deverell-DiFrenza was the owner of SwanSea. "No, not at all. Please come in."

Caitlin entered and cast an automatic, all-seeing glance around the room. The disorder on the serving table propelled her to the phone where she dialed a number. There were no pushbutton phones at SwanSea, only beautifully designed decorator phones that blended with each room's elegant decor.

"Please send fresh table linen and a carafe of coffee to room thirty-three." A magnificent emerald wedding ring set flashed on Caitlin's hand as she hung up the phone.

"That wasn't necessary," Liana said, "but thank you."

"You're more than welcome. I want my guests to have the best service possible."

Uncertain why Caitlin was in her room, Liana waved her hand toward the sofa. "Would you care to sit down?"

"No, thank you. I don't want to keep you. It's just that I heard about your accident last night, and I was worried."

"Don't be. It's really nothing more than a bad scrape."

"Are you sure?"

Liana smiled. "I use to get scrapes worse than this when I was a little girl. There was a big oak tree in our backyard in Des Moines that I couldn't resist climbing. Unfortunately there's that silly law about what goes up must come down. I came down a lot."

Caitlin nodded solemnly. "I'm familiar with that law. SwanSea has some great trees."

Liana grinned, feeling some of her tension fade. Caitlin, who had more money than Liana was ever likely to see in her lifetime, was one of the most down-to-earth people she'd ever met. "But the urge to climb that tree was nothing in comparison to my fervent desire to learn to roller skate. I spent hours on my skates out in front of our house. You know, I don't think I ever skated the full length of our sidewalk without falling."

Caitlin laughed. "Well, I'm relieved you weren't hurt more seriously. You could have been so easily, you know. I was very concerned last night when I heard about your fall, but I thought it would be best if I didn't bother you. But when I saw Clay Phillips downstairs this morning, having breakfast with one of his assistants, the lovely redheaded girl—?"

"Sara."

"Yes, and you weren't with them, so I decided to come up."

"I'm glad you did. It gives me the opportunity to tell you how beautiful your hotel is."

A strange expression came over Caitlin's face. "Hotel—yes, I guess it is." She grimaced. "I've spent months working to that end, but it's funny, I still don't see SwanSea as a hotel. I wonder if I'll ever get over the mind-set that this is my home and the people who've come here are my personal guests."

"Why should you get over it? I understand that SwanSea *was* your home. Besides, that attitude is exactly why you'll have a great success. Believe me. I've stayed in some of the finest hotels all over the world, but I've never been in one with more warmth and character than SwanSea."

Caitlin clapped her hands together with delight. "Wonderful. You've boosted my confidence a hundred percent, and I needed that. You wouldn't believe the problems that have cropped up in the last few days."

She'd believe the problems, Liana thought, but she didn't believe that Caitlin needed a boost of confidence. She radiated a strength and a happiness and a feeling that she could handle anything. Liana envied her.

Caitlin shrugged lightly. "Oh, well, I expected as much for the opening. And as long as my guests don't suffer, I don't mind." She clasped her hands together and eyed Liana intently. "Now, do you have everything you need?"

"Everything. Your staff is wonderful."

"I'm glad to hear it, but I don't want you to hesitate to call if you should need anything at all. If we don't have it, we will do our best to get it."

"I'll remember that," Liana said with a smile.

By late that afternoon, Liana was wondering if Caitlin could send out for a bottle of energy for her. She'd spent hours under the sun and hot lights in first one evening gown and then another. As they'd moved from one outdoor location to another, it had seemed to her that Clay had been unusually demanding. She understood, though. This was the first major assignment he'd done on his own without the supervision of Jean-Paul, and he wanted everything to be perfect.

But she longed for Jean-Paul. Together they had always made a certain magic on film, and they had an unspoken communication between them that had made any photo assignment pleasurable. Richard had been right in that at least.

"Hell, we've lost our light." Clay plowed his fingers through his hair, the lines of his body set with displeasure and tension. "All right," he said with a sigh. "That's it for today. I'll let everyone know the shooting schedule for tomorrow."

Liana retreated inside an aluminum-framed tent and slipped out of the green beaded gown she'd worn for the last series of shots.

Sara joined her and took the gown. "You were wonderful, Liana."

"Thanks," she said, giving the girl a smile. Although she hadn't met Sara before this trip, Liana thought she was very nice and eager to learn all aspects of the business. She plucked the hairpins from her hair. The tight coil at the base of her neck loosened, then opened, sending a shining, straight mass of wheat-colored hair down her back.

"How's your knee?" Sara asked.

"Not too bad." In truth, standing on it all day had made the dull ache of the bruise turn to a throb. "I'm thankful that I'm here to model evening gowns. The long skirts cover the bandage. If we were doing street-length dresses or bathing suits, *you* would have been the one out there in front of the cameras, with the reflectors throwing heat and light onto you."

Sara's eyes widened. "No way could I do a big assignment like this one. Besides, I'm really happiest behind the camera." She ran her hand over the gown, caressing the beaded work, then carefully hung it up.

Liana pulled on a pair of shorts and a tank top and breathed a sigh of relief at the cool comfort of the outfit. "Clay has done layouts with you before, hasn't he?"

"Only small stuff. Nothing on this scale. Are you going back to the hotel now?"

She should get off her knee for a while, Liana thought, but the prospect of an empty room was unappealing, and the beauty of the grounds was pulling at her. "I think I'll take a short walk. I'm a little stiff, and the exercise will feel good."

Sara laughed quietly. "Exercise never feels good. A hot bath is more my speed and that's just where I'm heading. Maybe I'll even be able to catch a nap before dinner. Have you heard? We have to dress for dinner."

Liana smiled. "Yes, I did hear that."

"But do you know why?" Sara asked as they left the tent.

"I guess I hadn't really thought about it. Why?"

"This is SwanSea."

"What?"

"I asked one of the *very* dignified employees why we had to dress for dinner, and I was told with extreme politeness that this is SwanSea." She grinned, then shrugged. "See you later."

Liana ended up at the gazebo that stood on the windswept point overlooking the sea. The gazebo was made of iron bent in fluid arabesques. A fresh coat of white paint and new green and blue cotton ducking covers for the bench cushions made it a lovely retreat, but Liana thought she sensed an air of sadness and loneliness about the gazebo.

She rested a knee on the cushion and leaned against the railing, reflecting that she didn't mind the strange atmosphere. Sadness and loneliness were emotions with which she was all too familiar. She was used to being by herself; she had long ago made the conscious decision not to get too close to anyone. And it had been years since she'd thought of the irony that one of the most visible women of the decade was also one of the most isolated.

The money she earned modeling gave her security. The sense that she earned her money through hard work gave her satisfaction. But she accepted only the assignments she wanted, and arranged her schedule to suit herself. And when she reached the point where the feel of people's hands on her was just beginning to penetrate through her mind block, she'd retreat to the countryside of France where she had a cottage and no one but Jean-Paul Savion had the address.

Her success had ensured her freedom from people and their demands; it was the main reason why her career was so important to her.

"You know what I remember most about your legs?"

She spun at the sound of Richard's voice, her heart beating wildly. He wore an icy blue shirt paired with taupe-colored slacks, and she'd never seen him look more virile and attractive. Or more dangerous.

He raked his gaze up the long length of her bare legs. "I remember how they seemed to go on forever," he continued, "and how tightly they gripped my waist when we made love. And when you climaxed—"

"Shut up, Richard."

His smile seemed almost genuine, she thought with a distant part of her mind, but she knew better. A smile was an indication of friendliness or affection. He felt neither of those things for her.

"You always did look nice in shorts," he said. "But then you've got the kind of body that shows off clothes to their best advantage. Still, I always liked you better without—"

"Shut *up*, Richard."

He bounded up the steps into the gazebo. Before she had time to prepare herself, he was beside her. Suddenly she felt trapped, as if there were no place for her to run. In fact, all she had to do was step around him and leave. She started to, but the sudden softness of his voice stopped her.

"Relax, Liana. Words can't hurt, you know. Not unless the person at whom they're directed cares, and you certainly don't." He waited a heartbeat, then asked in an even softer voice, "Do you?"

"No, of course not."

"No, I didn't think so." His gaze dropped to the bandage wrapped around her knee. "How is it?"

"Fine."

"Have you applied more antibiotic cream and changed the bandage as the doctor told you to?"

"Not yet."

"But you will, won't you?"

"Of course."

He threw a quick glance around the gazebo. "What are you doing here?"

She had been on the verge of leaving again, but this time it was the puzzlement in his voice that stopped her. "You mean at SwanSea?"

"No. What are you doing here in the gazebo? You're all alone. The sun is about to set; it will be dark soon, not to mention cooler." He waved his hand toward her. "And all you're wearing is that skimpy outfit."

There were reasons for everything he mentioned,

but she chose to tell him only one. "I love the sea. I have ever since the first time I saw it."

He drew closer. "When was that?"

She took a step away. "I guess the first time was when my father took my mother and me on a vacation to California." As always when she thought of her father, conflicting emotions besieged her. Unconsciously she stiffened her spine. "At any rate, I don't suppose it's so unusual for a girl who grew up in Des Moines, Iowa, to love the sea."

"No, I don't suppose it's so unusual."

His stare was analytical, his voice low-key, yet the friction in the air was palpable. She had the feeling that if she threw a match into the air between them, it would burst into flame spontaneously.

"It was always hard for me to picture you being from Des Moines," he said after a moment. "You're much too exotic."

"Des Moines was a wonderful place to grow up," she said, automatically defensive, though not directly answering him.

"But you left."

She shrugged. "I couldn't have gotten as far as I have in modeling if I'd stayed there. Pictures and spreads from my local modeling went to New York. Then my portfolio appealed to several designers in Paris. As luck would have it, one of the designers chose me for a runway show before any New York clients could line me up. The job in Paris was a gold-plated opportunity, and I took it." She'd had to. She'd been desperate for the money.

"I guess that pretty much must be the story of your life, right? Taking opportunities—no matter who gets hurt." He paused. "Or was I the only one you stepped on as you climbed your way to the top?"

"I have to go."

His hand encircled her arm as she moved past him. It was the contact of his hand on her skin more than his grip that halted her in her tracks. She gasped at the heat, at the hurt.

He released her immediately. "I didn't grab you that hard."

Silently, with an instinctive need to soothe, she rubbed her arm where he had touched.

Frowning, he moved a few steps away. After another puzzled glance at her, he fixed his gaze on the horizon. "So what's it like to have the world's greatest designers create one-of-a-kind gowns for you?"

"The gowns weren't designed for me," she said, happier about speaking of something that didn't affect her emotionally. "They were designed for SwanSea. Each designer was inspired by an aspect of SwanSea, whether it was a color, a texture, a pattern, or, with some, even just a feeling. Then they created a gown that would complement that aspect or conjure up the feeling that had inspired them."

"Maybe. At least that's what the press release said. But when they designed the gowns, they knew you were the model who would be wearing them. I'm willing to bet that a large portion of their inspiration came from you."

"The gowns aren't for me," she repeated firmly. "Any model could wear them. And they're to be auctioned off at the end of this two-week opening celebration. The proceeds will go to charity."

"Still, the ones I've seen you in so far look as if they'd been made solely for you. Especially the teal gown you were wearing last evening."

"You've seen me in other gowns? You saw me modeling today?" How could she have been unaware of him watching her? she wondered, disturbed at the thought.

"I caught an occasional glimpse of you here and there. It was hard not to. You seemed to be everywhere."

"I only remember three locations."

"Whatever," he said in a tone that expressed boredom with the subject, then took her by surprise by abruptly turning toward her. "Has it been worth it, Liana? Doing everything you've had to do to achieve your success?"

"Yes," she replied without hesitation, understanding that they were talking about two different things, but also understanding that it would make no difference if he knew. She'd left a deep scar in him. She was well acquainted with scars. She had her own to deal with.

Suddenly the imaginary match lit.

He reached out and grasped her face between the long fingers of his hand. "This face," he muttered. "This damnably beautiful face."

Her fragile shield of composure disintegrated with his touch, and in its place, a treacherous need sprang up, softening the urge to recoil and run. "It's ugly," she whispered.

"Yeah." He burst out with a hard laugh. "So ugly its image is permanently burned on the inside of the brain of every man who's ever seen it."

He stepped closer, his body brushing against hers, and her nerves reacted, coming alive, crackling with pleasure and pain. "You're exaggerating. There's nothing remotely attractive about me. My hair is board straight."

"It's thick, and silky, and just the right length to wind around a man's body."

Something molten and debilitating coiled through her. "My lips are too big—"

"They're full and sensuous and make a man fantasize about what it would be like to have his lips sealed to them for about a month."

"You're wrong." She stopped, cleared an obstruction from her dry throat, and tried again. "My eyebrows feather instead of going in a straight line."

"They make a man wonder if there's something not quite tame beneath that perfect control you project."

Somehow she managed to continue to draw air into her lungs, but the air seared her insides like a desert wind, leaving her struggling for breath. Frantically she searched for something else to say. "My eyes are an odd color and too far apart."

"They're arresting and impossible to look away from."

"My jaw is too strong."

"Yeah, but look how well it fits into my hand."

"My skin—"

"Catches all available light. I'm sure Savion has told you it's what makes you a dream to photograph. I'm sure he's also told you that your skin is so soft, stroking it makes a fire start in his belly. And, honey, I bet he strokes you a lot. He'd have to be crazy not to."

His thumb and finger had begun to rub her jaw, and as he spoke, they worked up to her cheeks, pressing harder and harder until it seemed as if he were trying to scrub something off her skin. She wasn't sure he was aware of the pressure he was exerting, but she was very aware she would be in serious trouble if she couldn't regain command of her emotions.

She tried to imagine that the two of them were doing a layout for sportswear or perfume, that he was a model with whom she was merely posing. It didn't work. Not at all.

"Your face," he whispered fiercely. "Your mouth, your eyes, your skin. Your *damned* sexy body."

"Richard . . ." The ruthlessness of his expression frightened her, excited her.

"It's all right," he muttered. "I'm immune."

And then he brought his mouth down hard on hers, and it was just as she had known all along. She couldn't block him out.

Kissing him again after all this time was like drowning. She felt as if a force were pulling her down, down, to somewhere deep and dark, where there was no escape. The force was Richard. She wasn't sure of the place. She wasn't sure if she cared.

She should fight, she thought hazily. There were reasons why she shouldn't be melting against him like she was. There were reasons why she should push against him and break away. He hated her. He wanted to hurt, then destroy her.

But what he didn't know was that she couldn't be hurt any more. She was all filled up with pain. And she'd destroyed herself eleven years ago when she'd walked out on him. Her career might be a success, but she was a complete and total failure. As a person. As a woman.

Nevertheless, she should fight.

His lips found the indentation behind her earlobe, and he brushed his tongue down the groove that ran behind her ear and partway down the side of her throat. A moan escaped her; a thrill shivered through her. Oh, Lord, he had remembered. She was very sure he'd had many women since their weeks together in Paris, yet he had remembered that one secret, special spot. He wasn't playing fair.

She should definitely fight.

But being in his arms after all these years overrode everything. The pleasure was simply too intense. All of her protective layers were peeling away one by one.

He made little sucking motions up her neck, tasting her, deliberately arousing her, and he had the satisfaction of feeling her go limp in his arms. At least in this one thing she hadn't changed. And neither had he, he thought angrily, as he felt himself grow hard with desire.

He slipped his hand beneath the tank top, and closed his hand around her breast. A shudder ripped through him. The *feel* of her hadn't changed either. As was true so long ago, her breast more than filled his hand. He'd always found something terribly erotic in the fact that she was so soft, yet so firm. And the way her nipples grew tight and stiff made him burn with an overpowering hunger.

In the past eleven years, he'd found no woman as intriguing, no woman nearly as satisfying. Liana was unique. And he wanted to break her neck because of it.

He caressed her roughly, but she was like a person deprived for too long of the essential elements of life. Nothing was too much. She wanted more and then more still. And so when he lowered her to her back on the softly cushioned bench she made no protest. And when he bent to pull her nipple into his mouth, she could only throw her head back at the ecstasy of the sensations that coursed through her.

"Richard, oh, Richard . . ."

"Yes," he said raggedly, his mouth wet on her breast. "Call my name. Make me think you want me."

"I do," she cried. "Oh, Lord, I do."

Ravenously he tugged at her nipple. The fact that he used neither gentleness nor care only heightened the intensity of the act and drew both of them toward the point where everything but the ecstasy would disappear. He switched his attention to the other breast. Half over her, he felt her hips lift. She'd probably done this sort of thing so often, it was second nature to her, he reflected, bitterness welling up in him. He wedged his knee between her legs and pushed upward. The sound that was ripped from her triggered a response in his mind, his heart, his gut.

His body blazed with passion, but his mind dispassionately sought caution.

He was a man torn, a man possessed. A man driven to have this one woman.

A man with a solitary unanswered question.

"You still respond like a woman who's giving herself totally to a man," he said roughly. "Are you, Liana? Are you willing to give yourself totally to me?"

His voice sounded as if he were far away from her, she thought, but that couldn't be. His weight was pressing her into the cushions, his body heat was burning through her clothes to her skin. "Yes."

He laved his tongue around a nipple. "You're lying."

She felt feverish, achy, and wasn't sure she had understood him correctly. "What?"

He nipped at her and heard her tiny cry. The roar of the ocean mixed with his heartbeat and thundered in his ears. She was like a siren, trying to lure him to his destruction with a bewitching sweetness and an insidious seductiveness.

The thing was, he'd been to hell and back and

lived to tell about it. There was absolutely nothing she could do to him.

He told himself this, and he believed it.

He shoved his hand beneath the hem of her shorts and the elastic edge of her panties until he found the moist warmth he was seeking. He almost lost control then, and for a moment, he forgot what he had been about to say. He plunged his tongue deep into her mouth, and lower, his fingers imitated the motion of his tongue.

The memory of what it was like to be inside her came rushing back, and he was gripped by a heat and need so intense, it seemed his life would be threatened, making him the liar.

"I want you," she whispered against his ear, forgetting time, place, and reason. "I want you so badly."

He drew a deep painful breath and tried to clear his head. Passion had never been their problem. Apparently it still wasn't. She could turn him on like no one else. But . . .

He jerked his hand from her shorts. Their faces were so close, their ragged breaths intermingled, but he didn't notice. He was too busy looking at the desire in her eyes.

"I could take you, couldn't I? Couldn't I, Liana?" he said louder. "Right here. Right now."

"Yes," she said on a sob and turned her head away.

Her answer fanned the flames inside him until he wasn't sure he could control them. But he *had* to reject her. It was the smart thing to do. "I was twenty-nine when we met. I'd had my share of women, but you were the hottest I'd ever had. I thought you were the most incredible thing that had ever happened to me. When I wasn't making love to you, I was thinking how lucky I was."

As he watched, her passion slowly faded to be replaced by bewilderment. And with the cooling of her passion, he felt stronger. Still, he couldn't quite make himself move away from her. "You were so sweet," he said, the memory thickening his voice in spite of his intentions. "I couldn't get enough of you. If there'd been some way to take you intravenously, I would have done it. What a high—a constant stream of you, pumping through my veins. If we'd stayed together long enough, I might have found a way." Abruptly he pushed away from her and sat up. "I guess I should really thank you. You saved me from becoming addicted to you."

Liana pulled the tank top down to cover her nakedness, but she stayed where she was, too weakened by what had just happened to move. "What are you saying, Richard?"

"I'm saying that I've been innoculated against you." His mouth twisted cruelly. "I may be the only man in the world who is. I wonder if science would be interested in using my blood to make a vaccine against you."

Her stomach churned sickeningly. She closed her eyes, certain she was going to throw up.

"What do you think, Liana? Should I volunteer my blood? I might even get the Nobel Prize." Her unresponsiveness didn't faze him. He felt driven, unable to stop the bitter, hateful words. "Another man might fall for the way you give yourself during lovemaking, but I'm in the unique position to know that you have no heart, no soul." At a small sound of distress from her, he bent and pressed a hard kiss to her lips. "Don't worry," he whispered. "I'm not saying we won't eventually go to bed together. There's nothing wrong with the purely physical as long as it's kept in perspective. Right?"

After a moment, she felt his weight leave the cushion, then heard the retreat of his footsteps as he left the gazebo. Tears slipped from beneath her lashes and slid slowly down her cheek, and her only thought was that she'd been right about this gazebo. There was an incredible sadness here.

Richard turned on the cold faucet and stepped into the etched glass shower stall. He didn't flinch as the icy water hit him. He braced his arms against the tiled wall, welcoming the frigid temperature as it washed over his body, numbing his body and his mind. He stayed and he stayed, until, when he finally turned off the water, he was satisfied that he couldn't feel a thing.

Three

Liana brushed her fingers across the brooch pinned to the bodice of her evening gown and wished herself anywhere but the dining room of SwanSea. She'd almost stayed in her room. After her encounter with Richard in the gazebo that afternoon, the last thing she had wanted to do was face a large group of people. Even now she could feel their curious stares, as harmful to her as physical blows.

Jewellike flower lamps by Tiffany lighted the room. The long graceful leaves of potted palms stirred ever so slightly in the gentle currents of air. In the background, a string quartet played pleasantly, soothingly. Startling white linen table-cloths draped tables ladened with glistening silver, gleaming china, and sparkling crystal. Tall white candles added their golden flames to the elegant ambience, and bowls filled with velvet-petaled roses emitted a faint sweet scent.

She had to get out of here.

"Are you all right, Liana?"

An unaccountable desperation was working in

her, urging her to bolt from the table, and it was only her years of discipline that came to her rescue. Calmly she looked across the expanse of white linen at Sara, and not even the merciless eye of a camera lens could have detected the effort it cost her. "I'm fine, thank you."

"It's my fault. I worked you too hard today," Clay said, sitting in the chair to her right. "After that fall you took last night, I probably should have canceled today's schedule. Jean-Paul will have my hide if he hears about this."

She reached over and patted his hand. "I'm getting tired of telling you people I'm fine. Just believe me. And about Jean-Paul, you know as well as I do how ruthless he can be when it comes to getting the pictures he wants. He would understand."

Clay's mouth twisted wryly. "You're right about him being ruthless—when it comes to his profession at any rate. Have some champagne. It will make you feel better."

In the hopes that he'd drop the subject of her well-being, she raised the fluted glass to her lips and let a small sip of the cool, bubbly wine slide down her throat. It felt good.

"Champagne seems to fit SwanSea, doesn't it?" asked Rosalyn, striking in a pale rose dress that grazed her ankles. "I mean the glamour of this place is incredible."

Steve shrugged his shoulders against the unaccustomed weight of a dinner jacket, then with a grimace ran a finger inside the buttoned collar of his white dress shirt. "This place is damned hard on your eyes, if you ask me."

"Hard on your eyes?" Rosalyn asked with disbelief.

"Everywhere you look, there's something fantastic. That sort of thing can damage your eyesight after a while." Still squirming uncomfortably, he crossed his long, blue jean-clad legs beneath the table.

Rosalyn laughed. "You can drop the jaded, world-weary act, Steve. I know better. I can't believe how lucky we are to be at this opening. The house isn't full yet, but by the night of the ball, I understand everyone who's anyone in New York society will be here. Liana, have you picked up any information about the socialites who are coming?"

Hearing her name, Liana pulled herself back from the distant place in her mind to which she'd retreated. She shouldn't have been there anyway. Richard had been there, and it had been springtime in Paris. "I'm sorry, what did you say?"

Sara, demure and lovely in a long, gold shirtwaist, used her champagne glass to gesture toward Rosalyn. "She's been busy picking up gossip."

Rosalyn suddenly gasped with admiration. "Look, Liana. There's that man who caught you last night when you fell."

She looked, not because she wanted to, but because Richard's very presence demanded that she do so. He was standing in the arched doorway, self-assured and at ease, carrying on a casual conversation with an attractive younger woman who stood beside him. She saw his gaze idly sweep the room, then stop cold on her and narrow. Something sharp pierced her heart. The candlelight blurred, the music dimmed.

"Who *is* he anyway?" Clay asked.

"Richard Zagen," she whispered. His mouth curved into a slow, hard smile, telling her he'd read her lips.

Her fingers sought out the brooch, its familiar textures and shapes acting as a worry stone. Odd, she thought, how this inanimate object could comfort her. But she'd loved it from the first moment she'd seen it—an exquisite lily with carved ivory petals, topaz stamen, and gold and green enameled stem and leaves.

"What a *beautiful* brooch."

The sound of a friendly voice gave Liana strength to tear her gaze from Richard, and she turned her attention to Caitlin who had just come up to their table. "Thank you."

"You're welcome." Caitlin gave her a smile, then addressed the entire table. "How is everyone tonight? Are you all enjoying yourselves?"

"Absolutely," Rosalyn said. "We've never had more luxurious working conditions."

"Usually we're on some atoll that isn't even on the charts," Steve mumbled, fidgeting in his chair.

"And that's in the dead of winter," Rosalyn added. "If the weather's cold, you can always find us on some beach. Tell me, is it true that the Trumps will be coming to the ball?"

Liana heard Caitlin laugh, but her reply to Rosalyn somehow blended into a muted white sound. Richard was no longer at the door. Lord, where *was* he? She cast a surreptitious glance around the dining room. He was here somewhere. The surface of her skin felt too exposed, her soul too unprotected, for him not to be.

Then she saw him seated at a corner table that gave him an unobstructed view of her. He was smiling at his dinner companion, and the woman seemed to be hanging on his every word. But much to Liana's dismay, she found it didn't matter that his attention was elsewhere. Richard didn't have to look at her to affect her. His mere presence made her feel battered and bruised, as if she'd taken another fall down the great marble stairway.

And it would have been much better for her if she had, she reflected. Instead she'd allowed herself to fall under Richard's spell, to be carried away by his kisses and caresses, to forget their past. Any one of those things had the potential to be fatal, and she'd done all three.

She should leave SwanSea. It would solve everything. She could fly to France and retreat for a while to her cottage. It would be so easy. She sighed, bringing herself to a mental halt. Unfortunately for her—at least in this instance—she was too disciplined, too professional, to leave an assignment.

"That is a stunning gown, Liana," Caitlin said. "Should I know the designer?"

"What?" she asked dumbly, then quickly recovered. Her dress was a deceptively uncomplicated midnight blue dress of silk and chiffon. The sheer material draped from its right lower side upward to the top left of the bodice. From there, a single sheer panel swept over her shoulder and dropped down her back to the floor-length hem. "The dress is by a friend of mine, but he's not well known yet."

"He will be soon though," Sara said in her quiet voice. "And every dress of his Liana wears in public increases the odds of his success."

"I can see that it would," Caitlin said thoughtfully. "You know, my sister-in-law, Angelica DiFrenza, might be interested in his clothes for DiFrenza's. She'll be here for the ball. I'll introduce you, and you can put them in touch."

"I'll be glad to," she murmured.

It was a sense of self-preservation that made her check to see if Richard was still sitting in the same place as he'd been when she had looked the last time. But her need to safeguard herself disappeared as her gaze collided with his. The heat and the hatred of his expression lacerated her, opening wounds she had worked hard to keep closed. She reached for her champagne glass. "Did your friend design the brooch, too, Liana?"

Liana took another cooling, sustaining drink before she answered Caitlin. "No, the brooch was a gift from another friend."

A frown of concentration knit Caitlin's brow as she stared at the brooch. "I just wondered. The lily design seems so familiar."

"I'm sure it does. It's of the art nouveau period."

"Do you know who the artist was?"

"I was told it was René Lalique."

"Really? That's very interesting. I just wish I knew why I think I've seen it before."

"Lalique must have used the lily as a theme many times, but with different variations."

"Yes, I guess you're right." Caitlin raised her head, and a smile suddenly lit her face. "Oh, how wonderful, my husband is finally here."

Everyone at the table followed her gaze toward the doorway and the handsome man with black hair and olive-toned skin.

Caitlin waved at him and mouthed, *I'll be right there,* to him. He nodded, and she turned back to the occupants of the table. "I wasn't sure he was going to make it tonight. He and his partner have had to be in Boston all week."

"Is that his partner with him?" Sara asked, indicating the tall, lean, sandy-haired man standing with Nico DiFrenza, his hands stuffed casually into the pants of his western cut evening suit. "He looks interesting."

Caitlin laughed. "Women usually use the word fatal in reference to him. And yes, that's Nico's partner, Amarillo Smith."

"He's wearing boots," Rosalyn said with slight amazement.

"Of course," Caitlin said. "Well, they're waiting for me. It was lovely talking with you. Enjoy your dinner."

Clay spoke for everyone. "Thank you, I'm sure we will."

"I wonder what she would have said if she'd seen my tennis shoes," Steve said after Caitlin left.

Rosalyn's eyebrows rose. "Not to mention your jeans."

Liana watched with a pang of envy as Caitlin's husband enfolded her in his arms and kissed her. "I'm sure she wouldn't have said a thing."

"She did seem nice, didn't she?" Sara said.

Liana unconsciously sought out Richard. To her dismay, his attention was still focused on her. "Is there any more champagne?" she asked.

Rosalyn tilted her head and stared at Liana. "I've never seen you drink on a photo shoot before."

Liana forced a smile. "But we're at SwanSea, and as you said, it seems proper."

"I agree," Clay said, summoning a waiter.

Dinner was almost over, but Liana couldn't remember eating a thing. It seemed to her that Richard had watched every move she had made, every breath she had drawn.

Several of the dining room doors that led out onto a large terrace were open. Occasionally she had seen the embroidered silk drapes billow as a breeze slid into the room. But even though no one else at the table seemed uncomfortable, she felt overly warm, disoriented, light-headed.

Music and conversation blurred into a muted

wall of noise and flowed over her without making an impression. She reached for her champagne glass and was surprised to find it empty.

"Let me refill that for you," Clay murmured, even while he was doing so.

She drank without acknowledging his courtesy. Was it guilt over Richard that was making her so edgy, she wondered. Or was it the need that, unbidden, rose up in her every time she saw him? *No.* She stopped that train of thought in its tracks. She would acknowledge the guilt, but not the need.

She'd lived with the guilt of her deceit for the past eleven years, and with the help of a strong system of defense mechanisms, she had survived.

But this need—she had to forget about it. Even though there had been many times when she had awakened aching for him over the years, her desire had always been easily quenched by the hard, cold realization that she had been dreaming and he wasn't there beside her and never would be again.

But she wasn't dreaming now. He was a short walk away from her, and she had learned this afternoon that she had no defense against him.

"I have to get out of here," she mumbled, pushing back the chair and struggling to her feet.

Clay jerked around, startled. "Liana, what's wrong?"

Her hand shot out to the high back of the chair to steady herself. "Nothing. I just need some air."

"Would you like me to go with you?" Steve asked.

Another time she might have smiled at his eagerness to leave the formality of the dining room. Another time she might have couched her rejection in a softer tone. But not this time, not with Richard staring at her from across the room. "No, I'd rather be alone."

• • •

Lights placed unobtrusively beneath shrubs and in grasses guided Liana along unfamiliar paths as she walked farther and farther from the house. She stumbled occasionally, but quickly regained her footing and kept going. She had no destination in mind. It was more a matter of going *away from* than *to*.

She finally stopped when she reached the edge of the cliff. Here, the ocean's roar was louder, the moon and stars brighter, the mood of the night blacker, more isolated. She drew a deep breath and felt herself sway.

"Be careful!" a deep voice said from behind her.

She turned quickly and almost fell. "Richard!"

He grasped her arms to steady her. "You're drunk."

What was the use of denying it? "The champagne was very good." And you, she thought, were completely unnerving. "What are you doing out here?"

"I followed you."

The idea that he had deliberately sought her out panicked her. Plus there were his fingers wrapped around her arms. She tried to break away from him, but his grip didn't ease. "What about the woman you were having dinner with? You just *left* her?"

He frowned as if he were having trouble comprehending her train of thought. "Margaret? She's my administrative assistant. We had some business to discuss, but she's back in her room working now."

She put a hand to her swimming head. "I thought you were here on vacation."

"I've never quite developed the knack of complete relaxation. Some people call me driven." A private thought firmed his mouth into a hard line. "Come away from the edge of the cliff, Liana. You might think it's the answer, but in the end, you wouldn't be happy with the way you looked smashed on the rocks below."

The ground seemed to be rising and falling beneath her feet. Her mind was having trouble operating in the midst of such dizzying motion. Richard was the only thing around her at the moment that was steady and unchanging. She had the greatest urge to hold onto him for dear life, but their past made that impossible. "What are you talking about?"

"Nothing important," he said, casually moving her back from the edge.

His hand on her bare arm was causing internal damage she might not be able to repair. "I really need you to take your hand off me, Richard," she said as clearly and as firmly as she could.

His brows rose, but he released her, then adopted an indifferent tone. "So, when did you become an alcoholic?"

The shock of the question nearly made her lose her balance. "What an incredible thing to say."

"Not so incredible when you consider how much you had to drink tonight."

"It was only champagne."

"I know, but I seem to remember that you never could drink much of it. One glass and you'd be light-headed. If I needed confirmation that you hadn't changed, I guess I have it."

"I guess you do," she said dully. Moonlight slanted over his face, its silver light emphasizing the cold set of his expression. He represented a great menace to her, but she found she couldn't look at him without wanting him. She turned away and fixed her gaze on the phosphorescent shimmer of the dark sea. "Why did you follow me?"

"It's easy to follow someone who looks like you do, Liana."

He moved closer, and then closer still, until she could feel the warmth of his hard body up and down her back, and a new type of intoxication invaded her bloodstream. She closed her eyes. "Go away, Richard."

He bent his head, put his mouth against her ear. "You know what else I remembered as I sat there and watched you tonight?"

His breath was warm on the delicate shell of her ear. She no longer heard the ocean's roar, only his voice, quiet and intimate. "I don't want to know."

"But I want to tell you. It's about that afternoon in Paris when we discovered another way to use champagne."

His words conjured up the day for her with clear, perfect recall. She swayed back against him, and he slid his arms around her waist. As a lover would do. Or as a man trying to set a trap for her.

"Remember, Liana? We ordered cases and cases of champagne. The waiters who delivered them to our room couldn't imagine how we were going to drink all of those bottles, just the two of us, and unchilled bottles at that. They didn't even try to hide how crazy they thought we were, did they? But we didn't care. Remember how we laughed?"

She remembered too well—the joy and the sunshine that temporarily had hidden the reality of why she was with him, the feeling on that afternoon that no one else in the world could possibly be experiencing the same intensity and passion as she was.

"When they left, we emptied the bottles into the bathtub, undressed, and got in."

He licked a spot on her neck, then kissed it. A shudder raced through her, and her head fell back against his chest. *"Richard."*

He went on, his words thicker, huskier. "We made love all afternoon. Looking back on it, I don't think it was so much the champagne that made me drunk as it was drinking it from your skin. I own several wineries now, but not one of them produces a wine that tastes half as good or as potent as what we bathed in that day."

Suddenly he spun her around, and the desire she saw burning in the gray depths of his eyes made her gasp and go weak at the knees.

"What do you think, Liana? Would you like to take a champagne bath with me again? We both know more now. We've had more experience. We could make that champagne boil."

She jerked away and lashed out at him, desperate to hurt him as he was hurting her. "How's your wife, Richard?"

He didn't even blink. "You mean my *ex*-wife? She's happy and healthy and living a very rich life with my money. Which was the whole idea in the first place."

She couldn't believe what she was hearing. "She married you for your money?"

"Of course."

"And you knew?"

He nodded, his gaze never leaving her. "Since I'd already experienced a relationship with deceit, I thought one without deceit might work. One where both parties knew what they were getting. Her, my money. Me, a hostess and sometime companion." He shrugged. "In the end, it was worth the money she wanted to get rid of her."

A chilling wind sent her gown swirling out around her, an undulating midnight blue cloud in a midnight black world. Her throat burned with emotion too raw to express. "I've got to go." She turned sharply and started off down the path.

"Wait."

She felt his hand close around her arm and whirled on him like a wounded animal. "Don't touch me! I can't stand it!"

Puzzlement scored his face as he stared at her. "I couldn't have hurt you, Liana."

That was really funny, she thought, but found she couldn't laugh. "Just leave me alone." She turned again, wanting to put as much distance between them as possible, but she didn't get very far before the heel of her shoe came down on a pebble and she stumbled.

Somehow Richard was there to catch her, disgust in his voice. "Lord, you can't even walk." He swept her up into his arms and started back toward the house.

A violent storm of turmoil closed in around her. His strength, his scent, his overwhelming masculinity—his trap had closed around her. "I can make it on my own," she insisted.

"Obviously not, Liana. You're drunk."

She was sure she was, but there was more than wine working in her. Her world was spinning out of control, she didn't know how to stop it, and suddenly she was too tired to try. She went limp against him, winding her arm around his shoulder and resting her head against his chest.

"There," he said. "That's better."

No, she thought. It wasn't better. It was simply the only choice she could make at the moment. She could detect no tenderness or caring in the way that he held her, but she was too weary to worry about his motives. "Can we just stop our hostility for tonight?" she murmured.

"A truce?" he asked mockingly. "What an imaginative idea."

The lights were brighter now; they were drawing closer to the house. She sighed softly, her breath exhaling against the strong column of his throat. "Can't you let it go? Even for a short while."

His arms tightened, pulling her even closer against him. "I don't know."

"Just for tonight. I can't fight you any more tonight."

"Then don't."

There was something in his voice that made her add, "I also can't make love with you."

"Who said anything about love, Liana? I can't recall that I did."

What was the use? she wondered despondently. She should have known better than try to reason with him, but she supposed being held in his arms had warped her judgment. In the future, she'd remember. Their past made reason impossible.

"Put me down, Richard," she said as they approached the back of the house. "I don't want anyone to see you carrying me."

"Worried that your glossy image will be destroyed if someone sees you drunk?"

"I'm not drunk." And she wasn't anymore. The wind and Richard had whipped all effects of the wine from her.

"Don't worry. No one will see you. By accident, I discovered a back route the other day." He shifted her weight slightly and opened a small rear door that led into one of the back halls of the house. Once inside, he carried her to a service elevator that transported them to the third floor. Only when they were outside her door did he allow her to stand.

"Well, here you are, more or less safe, more or less sound. For now." He waited for some sort of retort from her.

But she sagged back against the door and her sleepy eyes drooped closed. He frowned. Strands of her pale wheat-colored hair had come loose from their coil and lay in enchanting tendrils against her cheek and shoulders. Thick dark lashes threw shadows over the flawless, nearly translucent skin of her cheeks. Her breasts rose and fell above the low neckline of her gown as she breathed.

She made him furious.

Why the hell did she have to be so beautiful? And why was she so damned tired? And most of all, why, out on the bluff, had she screamed at him when he'd grasped her arms? The most obvious answer was that she was repulsed by his touch. Except, she had appeared traumatized, and he had been reminded of a small wounded animal trying to protect itself. "Where's your key, Liana?"

The sudden sound of his voice shattered the lulled state of suspension into which she'd fallen. Her eyes flew open, and she automatically reached into the bodice of her evening gown and pulled it out.

His hand made a fist around the metal warmed by her body, and his eyes darkened. "Do you always carry your key between your breasts?"

"When I don't want to bother with a purse."

He stared broodingly at her for a moment. "Would you flinch away from me if I touched your breasts?"

Their confrontation on the bluff had drained all her energies. The simple truth was the only possible answer. "Yes."

Holding her eyes, he lifted his hand and stroked a petal's outer rim of the lily pinned over her heart. The topaz center glimmered golden. "It might be worth it."

"You'd like to see me flinch?"

"Given my preference, I'd rather see you under me, hot as hell and wild out of your mind."

Helplessly, she shook her head. "Why do you say things like that?"

"Maybe because it's so damned much fun getting a reaction out of you."

"Fun? You're having fun?"

"Oh, absolutely," he said grimly. He inserted the key into the lock and opened her door.

The light beside the tall, silk shrouded bed cast a warm glow into the room. The bed and the oblivion it offered beckoned, but from experience Liana knew that sometimes even sleep wouldn't let her forget. She heard the door click closed behind her. Instinct told her he hadn't left.

"You're going to need help undressing." He walked up behind her and quickly, easily unzipped her dress.

She gasped and barely managed to grab the dress to her before it fell to the floor. Holding it tightly to her breasts, she felt exposed. She took several steps away from him, then swung around. "Don't ever do that again!"

He shoved his jacket aside and planted a hand on his hip. "You know, you're as confusing as hell, lady. This time, at least, I was only trying to help."

"Don't make a big thing out of it, Richard. I don't like to be undressed, that's all."

"Your men must hate that a lot, but then again, maybe it's just one more thing that fascinates them about you. I know you sure as hell have my attention. This afternoon you dissolved like sugar for me. Tonight, you can't even stand my hands on you."

"This conversation is pointless. You and I are pointless."

"Pointless, Liana? Well, you're probably right. But then what difference does it make when we're having so much fun."

She drew a deep, steadying breath. She had to get him out of her room before she broke down. "Richard, the past is past. It accomplishes nothing to dredge it up. I'm here to work. You're here for a holiday. I think it's best if we avoid each other."

"You came to that decision all by yourself, did you? Very good, sweetheart. There's just one thing. A small thing really."

She didn't want to know. That's why she couldn't figure out why she asked, "What?"

"I still want to touch your breasts, quite badly as it happens. And you might as well know something else, I don't want to stop there. You asked for a truce, Liana, but we haven't even really gotten started, and a cessation of anything between us is unacceptable to me at this point in time. *I'll* tell you when we'll stop. *I'll* tell you when we'll begin." His eyes glittered hard as diamonds as he raked his gaze over her. "Goodnight, Liana. Sleep well."

Four

Liana woke the next morning with a headache and a stiff knee. Neither was enough to keep her from the day's shooting; she couldn't ever remember missing work.

Today would be the first time.

After the tumult of yesterday, she simply wasn't capable of facing anyone, much less the camera. Projecting the cool, poised look she was known for would be impossible.

Clay would probably go up like a rocket when she told him, and although she wouldn't let his reaction change her mind, she dreaded what she was about to do. She reached for the phone and dialed Clay's room number. "Good morning," she said when he answered. "This is Liana."

"Good morning, Liana."

He'd been expecting her call—the strange impression flashed on and off in her mind like a light bulb. "Listen, I'm sorry, but I'm not going to be able to work today."

"Oh? What's wrong?"

He sounded very calm, very reasonable, she

thought, somewhat amazed. But then again, he probably knew to the ounce how much she'd had to drink last night since he'd been filling her glass. "Nothing is really wrong. I think I just need some rest."

"That's probably a good idea. Take it easy today."

"I feel really guilty about this delay, but—"

"Hey, don't feel bad. Fortunately our schedule has some flexibility built into it. Trust me, this won't hurt the shoot at all, and the crew will bless you."

She blinked. "Well, okay, then. Thanks, Clay. I'll work extra hard tomorrow."

"Just promise me you'll relax today."

"I will, and thanks again. Good-bye." She hung up the phone and gave a sigh of relief. The hardest part was over. Now all she had to do was decide how she was going to spend this day.

She needed to be alone, to repair her nerves and rebuild her mental strength, but finding space where she could be alone would be easier said than done.

To stay in her room all day would stifle her. And mingling with the guests at the hotel was out. She wouldn't be able to bear their stares, their attempts at conversation, their requests for autographs. No, she had to get away from the hotel.

She could take one of the rental cars and drive up the coast, but somehow exploring SwanSea's grounds appealed to her more, and she'd noticed that not many people were taking advantage of the grounds that lay beyond the pool house and the tennis courts. She quickly dressed, slipping a violet cotton camisole over her head and tucking it into the waistband of a violet and periwinkle circular skirt. With sandals completing the outfit and her hair in a thick braid down her back, she left the room.

• • •

In his suite, Richard disgustedly flung his razor into the bathroom sink and leaned toward the mirror to view the tiny amount of blood oozing from the nick on his jaw. Too much caffeine, he supposed. Now that he thought about it, he seemed to remember the doctor, during his last checkup, bluntly telling him to cut down on the coffee. Oh, well.

Splashing water on his face, he cleaned the last vestiges of shaving cream from his cheeks and throat, then reached for a towel. A minute later, he strode into the bedroom where he downed yet more coffee, and as a concession to his churning stomach, ate a cold piece of toast.

A fitful night's sleep had driven him from his bed early. He'd worked awhile, read the paper, and dressed. What now, he wondered, definitely edgy and restless.

He hadn't had a vacation in eleven years, and he was learning that relaxing was certainly easier said than done. As a matter of fact, it took a great deal of determination. SwanSea offered any number of activities, but somehow nothing was holding his interest.

Just being here was a social advantage, and the business contacts he could make, if he were so inclined, held great potential. The prospect of the art auction was also something to anticipate. Even though his collection was purely for investment purposes, he had developed something of an appreciation for art over the years.

Still, taking everything into consideration, he couldn't help but ask himself what the hell he was doing here.

Suddenly he laughed out loud—a cutting, self-mocking laugh that turned back on him—because, deep down, he knew exactly what he was doing here. He'd known since the first moment he'd learned Liana would be here.

He was set on a course which he could not alter and from which he could not deviate. And if destruction lay in his path, so be it.

He strolled onto the balcony and surveyed the grounds. A woman with a wheat-colored braid down the center of her back caught his attention.

"Wait up, Liana!"

Liana turned to look back toward the house and saw Steve hurrying to catch up with her. She sighed. She supposed she'd been lucky to get this far without someone stopping her.

"Hi," she said to him when he drew even with her. "Haven't you heard? You've got the day off."

He grinned. "I heard, but I made Clay say it to me twice just to be sure."

She laughed lightly. "So what are you going to do with your unexpected vacation?"

"I haven't decided yet." He glanced down at the toes of his aged tennis shoes, then over her shoulders, and finally looked at her. "Listen, Liana, there's something I want to tell you."

"Okay," she said, wondering at his uneasiness. She had known him for about a year now, and normally, Steve was the epitome of an easygoing, self-confident young man.

"It's about your accident."

"What accident?" she asked blankly.

"When you fell down the stairway."

"Oh. Okay, what about it?"

He planted a hand on one narrow jean-clad hip. "Well, I've been thinking about it. At first I thought I must have inadvertently brushed against the light in some way to make it fall, but now I'm not so sure. I think it's possible that the light could have been rigged to fall."

Her eyes widened in surprise. "Why would anyone do that?"

He shrugged. "I don't know, but I checked out the light and one of its legs . . . Well, it just looks possible, that's all." He shrugged again. "I felt you needed to be aware that maybe the accident wasn't an accident after all."

"That doesn't make sense. What would anyone gain by causing it to fall? Everyone involved wants this shoot to be a success."

"That's true," he admitted grudgingly.

She lay a hand on his shoulder, "Steve, you need this day off more than I do."

"Maybe, but do me a favor and be careful. And you might spend some time thinking about who would like to see you hurt."

She shook her head. "I don't have to think. There's no one."

"Liana—"

"Steve, I appreciate your concern, but this wonderful place must have your imagination working overtime. I know it does mine."

He hesitated, then broke into a reluctant grin. "I guess you're right. Sorry, I didn't mean to upset you."

"You didn't. In fact, it makes me feel good that you were worried about me. But enough's enough. Go have a good time. Lord knows, Clay will work us hard enough tomorrow."

"You're right about that. Okay then, see you later. Just don't take any more falls."

"I promise."

Liana watched Steve walk back toward the house, then for some unexplainable reason, she lifted her gaze to a third-floor balcony. Richard stood there, watching her.

Her mind went blank, instinct took over. She turned and ran.

• • •

Leonora Deverell. Born 1877. Died 1898.

Liana lightly brushed her fingers over the letters, the only decoration on the small, simple, boxlike house that was Leonora Deverell's crypt. An oversized, heavy-looking concrete urn stood to the left side of the doors, empty. There should be flowers in it, she thought.

She knew from reading various articles on SwanSea that Leonora Deverell had been SwanSea's first mistress, and she seemed to recall that Leonora had been seventeen when she had married the wealthy, powerful Edward Deverell. A year later, her son, John, had been born. Then three years later, Leonora, after a sudden, brief illness, had died.

"How sad," she murmured.

"What's sad?" Richard asked.

She slowly turned, accepting completely that he was there. Running from him would have been an invitation to a man like Richard, and she'd called herself a fool many times during the past two hours for doing just that. But if she'd learned one thing over the years, it was that once something had happened, it couldn't be undone.

She had known he would come. In a way, she'd been waiting.

And where he was, there was danger for her.

With pulses racing, she met his gaze squarely. "What took you so long?"

He smiled. "SwanSea is a pretty big place, and by the time I got downstairs, there was no sign of you."

That's how she'd wanted it. She'd struck out blindly, away from the people, away from him. She'd walked across rolling green meadows dotted by wild aster and goldenrod. Bluebirds and blackbirds had swooped above her, darting between tall pines and majestic firs. At one point, two white-tailed deer darted across her path. She'd been enchanted by everything she saw, but she hadn't remained at any one place for longer than a few minutes. Leonora's crypt had been the only sight that had enticed her to come closer, to linger.

She should have kept moving.

"So how did you find me?"

"I looked in the most isolated places."

A nod acknowledged his discernment.

"So what do you find so sad?" he repeated.

"The fact that Leonora Deverell died at such a young age."

"It happened over ninety years ago, Liana."

"I don't care how long ago it happened, it's still sad. Leonora had a little boy and a husband who loved her very much." All the things she as a young girl had once yearned for, but had had to face that she would never have.

"How do you know her husband loved her?" he asked with amusement.

She shrugged and conceded, "It's an assumption."

"Based on what?" When she didn't answer, he went on, "I'm not trying to get into an argument with you, Liana. I'm just really interested in what has given you the idea that a man you never knew loved his wife."

She was sure his reasons for asking *were* argumentative, but in this instance, she didn't care. Perhaps if she put her feelings into words, it would help her understand why she was so drawn to this forlorn, forgotten place. "Well, first of all, Leonora was the first Deverell to die after SwanSea was built, so Edward had a choice of where he could locate the family cemetery. He placed her crypt as far away as possible from the house so that he wouldn't have to see it and be reminded of his pain."

"I don't know many people who would place a cemetery where they could look out the windows of their house and see it," he said dryly. "It's just too depressing."

"Maybe. But look where the rest of the family plots are." With a wave of her hand, she indicated a larger, more impressive crypt and several tall, elaborately carved gravestones placed some distance away. "He kept Leonora's apart."

He cocked an eyebrow. "Because he thought her so special?"

"I think so."

"Then, why is his crypt bigger than hers?"

"Her death was unexpected. The workmen would have had to throw this up literally almost overnight." She poked at the base of the crypt with her toe. "See? The masonry is crumbling. Shoddy workmanship. And look at this." She reached for the big heavy lock on the two doors and tugged. "This is almost rusted through. A good tug would break it."

"*Why* are you so interested in this place?"

"I don't know," she said, equally baffled. "SwanSea has such a unique character and atmosphere to it. I sensed sadness in the gazebo, and here I sense tragedy." Her head turned in the direction of the house, though she couldn't see it. "There have been times of shadows as well as times of sunlight here."

His amusement took on an edge of fascination. "Are you normally so sensitive to places?"

She shrugged. "I can't remember another place

affecting me as much. It's almost as if I were familiar with SwanSea before I ever came here."

He gazed at her, baffled. "I would never have thought you such a romantic."

"A romantic?" She shook her head. "I'm definitely not." The two most important men in her life—her father and Richard—had seen to that. They had extinguished all traces of the starry-eyed dreams in her and in return had brought her immeasurable heartache. She glanced back at the crypt and the markings on it. "Leonora. It's a pretty name, don't you think?"

"Yes, but then so is Liana."

He trailed his fingers down her cheek. The touch was so light, she barely felt it, yet small frissons of heat coursed through her, causing equal parts pain and pleasure. How on earth could she have gotten so caught up with the life of a long dead woman, she wondered suddenly, when her own life demanded such energy and effort from her?

"I looked up the name Liana once," he said. "It's from a French word meaning to bind, to wrap around—you know, sort of like a creeping vine that strangles the life out of something. I remember thinking at the time how appropriate the name was for you."

Color flushed her skin. He just wouldn't let up. "My mother chose my name. She was French and died when I was very young."

"I didn't know that. But then if I tossed everything I *don't* know about you into the Seine, the river would flood Paris."

She had begun to feel an oppressive weight, and it had nothing to do with the cemetery. With no particular direction in mind, she began to walk, and he fell in beside her.

"Is your father alive?" he asked.

"No, he's dead now too." What irony, she thought, that he didn't know. But then again, what did it matter? She was all alone, and that was the way she liked it. She didn't want to be bound to anyone ever again. Most of all, she didn't want to be responsible for anyone else's pain. She glanced at him. He'd obviously learned his own protective defenses, and they appeared quite formidable. There didn't look to be a soft, unprotected place in him. She would be willing to bet that he allowed nothing to affect him emotionally.

They had both learned well. How very pathetic.

Suddenly she wondered if he had anyone close to him. "What about your parents? I don't believe you ever mentioned them."

"They're alive and happily retired."

"Retired from what?"

"My father owned a drugstore in Chicago. He worked hard all his life, but never could seem to get anywhere."

"Did it ever occur to you that the one drugstore might be all he wanted?"

He slipped his hands into his trouser pockets and bent his head, studying the ground in front of him as they walked. "Just lately it has."

"But you were unable to understand that when you were younger?"

"I'm still not sure I do entirely. I seem to be driven to acquire. Businesses. Art." He cut his eyes to her. "Other things."

"Do you think this drive stems from the fact that your father owned only one drugstore?"

He hesitated. "Partly." Then he added, "I've bought my parents a place in Florida. They're content." He seemed to shrug, then his head came up and he looked at her. "So why aren't you working today? Did you wake up with a headache?"

"Yes," she said, deciding to let him think she had a hangover. It was easier to go with his perception of her than fight it. All at once, a sense of desolation swamped her. The sad ending to Leonora's promising young life. Richard's festering hatred. Her own interminable sadness. It was all too much.

Abruptly, she changed directions and headed back toward the house. With Richard doggedly following her footsteps as he seemed bent on doing, she thought grimly, it would be better to be around people. Hopefully he would soon lose interest in her. Maybe he would even come to understand that it would be better for him to put their past behind him. As she had.

Sure, Liana. Sure.

She didn't believe for a minute that Richard had lost interest in her, Liana reflected the next morning. It was more as if he had put her on hold while he spent the afternoon playing golf. But he had been in the dining room last night, again with his attractive assistant, Margaret, and he had watched her every bit as intently as he had the night before. This time she coped without the champagne.

And now this morning, as early as it was, a crowd of people had gathered on the front steps of SwanSea, the first site of the day's shooting. Liana, dressed in a wrapper, sat before a makeshift table while Rosalyn laid out makeup, combs, and brushes.

Usually by this time in a day's shoot, her concentration was firmly in place. This morning, though, her thoughts were scattered. Leonora and her lonely resting place still bothered her and she didn't know why.

She chided herself. What a foolish thing to get upset about. She was being far too impressionable, too open to sentiment. It wasn't like her, and she needed to put a stop to it immediately.

She glanced up at the impressive facade of SwanSea. There was no doubt that it was magnificent, but she couldn't help wondering how Leonora had felt about SwanSea as a home. Living in a small, cozy house as she did, she would have a hard time viewing such a huge place as a home. Had it been just as overwhelming to Leonora as a seventeen-year-old bride? All at once she remembered another Leonora—

"Which dress is first, love?" Rosalyn asked her.

"What? Oh, the gold."

"I saw that one," Rosalyn said, reaching for the pot of foundation. "It's gorgeous, but then all the gowns are. I've overheard several ladies plotting their strategies for the auction."

Liana smiled. "It should be interesting."

Rosalyn applied a light base of foundation to Liana's cheeks, then a cream rouge. "You think we'll see any cat fights?"

"Here? No way. SwanSea is much too dignified."

Rosalyn made a sound halfway between a snort and a laugh. "Listen, sweetie, women and their love of beautiful clothes are the same no matter where they are. You mark my words. It's going to get down and dirty at the auction, and I for one can't wait." She broke the seal on a new jar of loose powder and screwed open the top, then she dipped a puff into the powder and held it toward Liana's face.

But Liana turned toward Sara, who was sauntering up to them.

"Clay's ready for you, Liana."

Liana smiled. "Thanks, Sara. I won't be much longer."

Rosalyn peered at her own image in the mirror. "We're leaving her hair straight for this shot," she said to Sara and idly dusted a sprinkling of powder over her own face. "All I have to do is brush it."

"Okay, I'll tell Clay. You know what? He's in a good mood. He should take more days off. If you call taking pictures of me a day off."

Rosalyn laughed. "Sounds like a busman's holiday to me."

"And for you, it doesn't sound like a day off," Liana said. "Besides, I thought you didn't like to have your picture taken."

"I don't, but it was all in fun. I even got to wear some of your designer gowns."

"Really?"

"Oh, don't worry. I was very careful with them."

"Sara, you don't have to reassure me. They're not *my* gowns."

Suddenly Rosalyn made a sound of pain, dropped the puff, and clutched at her face.

Liana looked up at her. "Rosalyn, what's wrong?"

"My face," she gasped. "It burns!"

Alarmed, Liana jumped up and guided Rosalyn into the chair. Even as she did, she could see red blisters rising on Rosalyn's face. "My Lord, she must be having some sort of allergic reaction. Sara, go see if there's a doctor registered."

"It's the powder," Rosalyn cried.

"Try not to touch yourself." Liana glanced frantically around and spied two ladies standing nearby. "Quick, run into the hotel and tell them we need cold, wet cloths immediately."

Steve came rushing up. "Sara yelled that something's wrong with Rosalyn as she raced by. What is it?"

Liana took one look at the worsening blisters on Rosalyn's face. "God, Steve, go call an ambulance. Now!"

Fifteen minutes later, Liana was watching the ambulance with Rosalyn in it roar off. "I need to be there for her," she said to no one in particular. "I'd better get dressed."

"Just a minute." Steve restrained her with a hand on her arm. "I heard you tell the paramedics that she'd had an allergic reaction to face powder. What exactly happened?"

"I'd like to know that myself," Richard said, coming up to them.

Her already distressed state was worsened by the sight of Richard. Intellectually, she knew that he was staying here at SwanSea. She was even on the alert against a sudden appearance by him. But she still couldn't get used to *him*—the flesh and blood presence of the man.

"I'd like to hear the story again, myself," Clay said, joining them.

Agitated and anxious to be with Rosalyn, Liana gazed at the three men around her. "I've already told you. She had an allergic reaction to the face powder."

Clay walked to the table behind them and picked up the still open jar. The paramedics had peeled off the label that listed the ingredients and had taken it with them. "Is this what she normally uses?"

"Yes, except normally she uses it on me, not on herself."

"Had she put any on you yet?" Richard asked, scrutinizing her face with narrowed eyes.

"No, she was just about to."

"What about when we last worked day before yesterday?" Steve asked. "Did she use it on you then?"

"No," she said, exasperation and impatience giving the word emphasis. "It was a new jar. She had just broken the seal."

"Could it have been tampered with in some way?" Richard asked.

"I don't see how," Clay answered, eyeing the seal that still lay on the table.

"And I don't see why," Liana said. "Look, it was an allergic reaction, plain and simple. Sometimes it just happens."

"Maybe something went wrong at the factory with the batch," Steve said.

Clay nodded. "I know a chemist I can send this to for an analysis. I'll take it into town right now and get it off to him."

"Fine. Do what you want. But I'm going to the hospital and see about Rosalyn."

Richard caught up with her just inside the massive front doors of SwanSea and grabbed her upper arm. "Wait a minute. You shouldn't go just yet."

She looked down at his hand on her arm, and he immediately released her. "Rosalyn is my friend, Richard. We've worked together for quite some time, and I want to be there for her."

"I understand that, but I also can see how shaken you are."

She wrapped her arms around herself. "It was an awful thing to watch happen."

"It would have been even worse to have it happen to you."

"Hearing that isn't helping me, Richard."

"Okay, okay. All I'm saying is that you should

give yourself some time before you drive into town."

She had thought all hope long dead in her, but she found herself saying, "It almost sounds as if you're concerned about me."

He stiffened; his voice mocked. "I just want to make sure you stay in one piece until we go to bed together."

Anger and hurt whipped color into her cheeks. "It's not going to happen."

"It has to, Liana."

She felt a cold shiver that affected her like heat. "Look, believe whatever you like, but I have to see about Rosalyn now.'"

"Then, I'll let you go. For now."

Five

The designer gown arched through the air, a beautiful streamer of shiny sequins and orange and gold chiffon.

Sara caught the gown, her eyes wide with astonishment.

Liana's mouth twisted wryly, knowing what the younger girl was thinking. Anything less than careful handling for such a gown would be called sacrilege by some. "Sorry. Clay took so long with that last shot, I'd begun to feel like the dress was plastered to me. I had to get it off. I didn't harm it, did I?"

After a brief inspection of the gown, Sara shook her head. "The gown's fine." She began to fold the one-of-a-kind creation with tissue paper. "Clay's been hell on wheels the last two days, hasn't he?" she asked, darting a glance at Liana.

"He's just trying to do the best possible work he can." Why was she defending him, she wondered as she reached for her jeans and a T-shirt. Clay had been almost unbearable to work with, pushing her and everyone else to the limit.

With the breakneck speed she had learned backstage at runway shows, she threw on her clothes. She wanted to get *away* from SwanSea. Nothing had gone right since she had been here, but then in all fairness, she had only herself to blame, not SwanSea. She had let imagination and emotions rule, and as a result, she'd had control over almost nothing that had happened.

She could pack up and go home, she thought for the one hundredth time, and as always, she discarded the idea. There was something keeping her here, and it was time to admit to herself that it was something that went beyond her feeling of responsibility for the assignment.

The obvious answer was Richard, but unable to cope with the volatile repercussions of that particular idea, she rejected it. Suddenly the image of the small concrete burial house on that windswept hill came to her. How very odd, she thought. Was she losing her mind?

"I can understand Clay trying to do a super job," Sara was saying, "but nothing any of us has done has been good enough for him."

It was true, Liana reflected. Under normal circumstances, she could have coped, but these circumstances were anything *but* normal. The past two days had been hard on her, both physically and mentally. She had tried time after time to retreat into her mind, but all her usual blocking devices had proved useless. Too many hands had touched her. Too many people had stared.

Today, it had reached the point that if Clay had told her to strike one more pose or to smile one more time, she would have cracked. As it was, she was hanging on to her composure by a thread.

With cream and tissue, she wiped off every last bit of makeup, then quickly ran a brush through her hair.

"Are you all right?" Sara asked abruptly.

No, she thought. She was far from all right. "Of course. Why wouldn't I be?"

"It's just that you've looked pretty frazzled since we've been here."

The younger girl seemed so solemn, Liana had to grin. "Are you afraid you're going to have to step in for me?"

Sara started. "Goodness no! I know what a professional you are. It would take something pretty awful to keep you from work."

Funny, Liana thought. Lately, she'd been thinking that it would take very little. The idea of retiring was becoming more and more desirable. "Well, don't worry. I have every intention of finishing this shoot. Now I'd better be on my way."

"Where are you going?"

"Into town to visit Rosalyn."

"You saw her yesterday, too, didn't you?"

Liana nodded.

"I've been meaning to get in to see her myself, but I've been so busy. Tell her hello for me, will you?"

"Sure will."

The sun was setting as Liana walked briskly toward the parking lot. Over the years, she'd found that an engrossed expression and a purposeful stride would deter all but the most ardent of her admirers. And it almost worked.

She was nearly to the rental car when she heard Richard ask, "You're certainly in a hurry. Is there a fire somewhere?"

Her heart leaped and an inconsequential thought

fluttered through her head—she certainly couldn't categorize Richard as one of her admirers.

She turned and, as always, became momentarily helpless at the sight of him. They hadn't spoken to or seen each other in two days, but she had known he was still at SwanSea. She had actually *felt* his presence. And feeling him without seeing him had been irritating, maddening, and had made her very, very skittish.

He smiled. "Missed me?"

"Have you been gone?"

Her pose of arrogance made her beauty that much more remarkable, and he felt a quickening of warmth deep in his gut. "That's good, Liana. Very good. No, I've been right here."

"Really? I can't remember seeing you."

"That's because I've been closed up in my suite. Something came up with one of my companies, and I've had a series of meetings that have lasted well into the night."

"Everything all right now?" Why in the world was she asking? It wasn't as if she cared.

"Everything's fine," he said. "Where are you going?"

She wasn't used to accounting to anyone for her time. But she had told Sara, and she would tell him if it would get her away from him quicker. "I'm going into town to see Rosalyn."

"Your friend who used the face powder, right? How is she?"

"I'm glad to say she's getting better every day."

"That came very close to being you in the hospital, you know. Have you thought about that?"

Of course she had. And the idea had stolen several hours of sleep from her. "It was a freaky thing to have happened. Fortunately Rosalyn didn't suffer that much. They were able to stop the burning almost immediately, and the doctor is certain that the blisters won't leave disfiguring marks."

"How long will the blisters last?"

"About a week. They'll leave red marks for a little while longer, but they say there are salves that will help the discolorations."

"Wasn't it lucky she put that powder on her instead of on you?"

She crossed her arms over her breasts. "Lucky for me, not for her. I feel awful for her."

"I'm sure everyone does, but still, the shoot hasn't been held up, has it?"

She sighed. She would answer this last question, she decided, and then she'd go. "No, it hasn't. I've been doing my own makeup, and Sara's helped when I've needed her. Clay's talked of flying someone in from New York, but I don't know whether he will or not."

"At least he won't have to fly in a new model. That really would have screwed things up, wouldn't it?"

Her brow furrowed. "Is there something you're trying to say, Richard?"

He tilted his head to one side, studying her. "Actually I wasn't. Normally if I want to say something, there's no *trying* about it." Suddenly an altogether unexpected teasing glint came into his eyes. "Although now that I think about it, have you considered the possibility that someone's after your job?"

Steve had told her he felt it possible that the light could have been rigged to fall—the light that had initially distracted her and led to her tumble down the marble stairway. If Richard hadn't been there to catch her, she could have suffered broken bones or even much worse. Then they would have had to replace her or cancel the assignment, which they wouldn't do. She had talked Steve out of the notion, but what if—*no*. It just couldn't be true. There was simply no one she could think of who would want to harm her.

She looked up at Richard and saw him watching her intently.

"Where were you just then?"

The question, gently asked, almost took her off guard. Almost. "Nowhere."

He cocked his head to the other side as if viewing her from another angle might show him something he hadn't seen before. "I've missed you."

An incredulous look spread across her face. "Missed me? You mean you've missed taunting me."

"You're absolutely right," he said. What gentleness there had been in his tone was gone now. He moved closer, his body pushing her back against the car. "It hasn't been all taunting, has it? I mean I have followed through once or twice. And by the way, there's something you should know. Up to now it has been merely a warm-up."

She felt his arousal press into her, and heat flared low in her stomach. "For God sakes, Richard, we're in the middle of a parking lot!"

"We could go to your room if you like. Or mine. Or that garden over there."

She pushed against him. "I've already told you that I'm on my way into town."

"You could change your mind. You've done it in the past."

"Leave me alone, Richard."

"I'm afraid that's impossible. Only the fact that I've been so busy has kept me from coming to your room."

An unwanted excitement sprang to life in her. "Dammit, Richard—"

"One morning I found myself outside your room at four A.M." The desire in his voice stoked the fire growing inside her. "You'll never know how close I came to bribing someone to open your door for me."

"The staff here is too well trained," she said, a tinge of desperation in her tone. "They wouldn't have accepted a bribe."

"For the amount of money I was willing to pay, Liana, *someone* would have accepted. You see, I wanted you very badly that night, as badly as I want you now."

She stifled a moan. "I've got to go."

"There's no need to run," he said, his voice husky, his lower body rubbing against hers. "Our going to bed together would involve only pleasure this time. There would be none of those sticky, complicated emotions that got in the way before."

She couldn't look away from him. He was hard, heartless, and bitter, and at the same time, he radiated a masculinity and a magnetism that absolutely undid her. And always, swirled between these two realities like the icing between two layers of cake, her memories of him as he had been in Paris seduced her. She should guard herself against him, and Lord knows she had tried . . .

She loved him. It was at that moment as she gazed up at him that she knew. Dear heaven, she *loved* him!

The thought sent terror clear through to her bones. She shoved him away and wrenched open the door. Quickly she slid into the car, pulled the door closed, and started the engine.

Richard remained where he was, disturbed because she had gotten away from him before he was ready to let her go and vaguely troubled because he couldn't entirely explain her abrupt behavior. There had been an expression on her face—

In the next moment, he instinctively jumped to the side as her car hurtled past him, though the car hadn't been aimed at him. With increasing speed and squealing tires, she drove out of the parking lot and down the long drive.

Richard's gaze remained on Liana's car as it receded into the distance, and he didn't notice that a man had walked up to him until he spoke.

"Was that Liana Marchall who just drove out of here like a bat out of hell?"

Tense and worried, Richard snarled at him. "Yeah, why?"

The man's brows lifted in mild reaction. "No reason. It's just that I hope she's not going to be driving like that all the way into town, that's all."

"Why?"

"I just came from that direction. Apparently a construction truck lost part of its load. There's all kinds of junk—nails, boards, cinderblocks—strewn over the road for about a quarter of a mile."

"Damn!" Richard was nearly to his car when he thought to yell over his shoulders, "Thanks for the information."

She knew she was driving too fast, but she couldn't seem to make herself care enough to slow down. She was too keyed up, too disturbed, and she lay the blame solely at Richard's feet. She couldn't look at him without things happening inside her.

Needs. Fears. Wants. Guilts. Passion.

She had been in a constant state of mental confusion and emotional turmoil for days now.

A field stretched to her right, and on the other side of the road, a cliff dropped some distance to the rocks and ocean below it. The wind had her hair flying about her head and into her face and eyes. Impatiently she brushed at her face and was vaguely surprised to find her fingertips come away dampened with tears. She choked back a sob.

She felt as if she were fighting a losing battle. Every time she saw Richard, she had the urge to go into his arms and have him hold her forever. Then in the next minute, she would want to run as far as possible from him. By turns she would have to fight the urge to beg his forgiveness, and bite her tongue to keep from telling him to go to hell.

Now she realized she was in love with him, in fact had never stopped loving him.

Oh, Lord, it all seemed so futile. What was she going to do?

She had driven over the debris before she realized it. The steering wheel jerked in her hands. Then she heard the slap of the rubber of her left front tire—*whop whop whop*—as it hit the asphalt.

The car veered out of control and into the left lane. Adrenaline surged in her veins. Frantically she jammed her foot against the brake pedal. The car went into a slide, turning sideways, skidding toward the edge of the cliff.

Just catching up to her, Richard went cold with fear as he saw what was happening. Even worse for him, there was absolutely nothing he could do to help her. To his horrified eyes, her car seemed to move in slow motion. It floated across the road and onto the gravel surface of the road's shoulder as it headed smoothly, yet with deadly certainty, toward the cliff's edge.

The car came to a stop. Liana's eyes were squeezed tightly shut and stayed shut until she felt sure the car wouldn't move again.

When she finally opened them, she looked out over the hood of her car and saw nothing but sky and open space. Very carefully, she drew in a deep breath. She glanced out her right window. Following the line drawn by the cliff's edge, she judged that all four tires were on solid ground. With an exclamation, she dropped her forehead to the steering wheel.

Richard jerked the passenger door open and hauled her out of the car. "Dear God, Liana! Are you hurt?"

"No." She pressed her fingers to her forehead. "What are you doing here?"

"I followed you."

A wave of dizziness washed over her. "You're really going to have to stop doing that."

His hard gaze took in her ashen face and her eyes filled with shock. The idea that she'd been frightened, that she'd nearly gone off that cliff, made him absolutely crazy. "It's a damned good thing I did follow you."

"Why?" She looked at him again, still puzzling over why he was here. "You didn't do anything to help."

That she was right made him all the more angry. "You crazy fool! What were you trying to do? Kill yourself?"

"No, Richard, I'm sure I can leave that to you." She congratulated herself on her quick comeback.

"You damn sure can if you pull this kind of a stunt again."

A wave of nausea came and went. Maybe it hadn't

been such a good answer after all. "One of my tires went flat."

"No kidding." He uttered a curse and pulled her against him. "Dammit, Liana, you're shaking."

She hadn't noticed. And now all she could focus on was the heat engendered by being in his arms. For the moment, she allowed herself the heat. She needed it.

He waited until he could feel the tremors in her body subside, then gently cupped her jaw and tilted her face up so that he could study it. "Are you really all right?"

"Yes." Moistening her dry lips with a sweep of her tongue, she stepped out of his grasp. "Thank you."

Staring at her in the growing darkness, he searched for some sign of what she was feeling. But it was like a beautiful curtain had come down over her, concealing all emotion. Recalling those terrifying seconds when he had watched her car skid out of control toward the cliff, he had the strangest urge to shake her. He couldn't remember ever being as scared as he had been at that moment. On some level, he was still scared. *He had to take some action.*

He strode toward the car, reached in the open door and wrenched the keys from the ignition.

"What are you doing?" she asked.

He slammed the door shut and locked it. "We'll leave it here. I'll send someone from the hotel to change the tire and drive it back."

"I can change the tire," she said, the protest automatic.

"So can I, Liana, but I'm not going to and neither are you." He grasped her arm and forcefully helped her into the passenger seat of his car.

From her point of view, it wasn't a second too soon—her strength had just deserted her.

Music drifted out the opened window of the main salon, rose like warm, soft air, and entered Richard's bedroom through his open balcony doors. He glanced at the bedside clock. Ten-thirty. After-dinner drinks were being served downstairs. People were laughing, dancing, enjoying themselves, but he wasn't tempted to join them.

Nerves were layered on top of nerves. Muscles were coiled to the point of pain. He craved something, but he didn't know what.

Liana was just down the hall.

He gnawed on a thumbnail, restless, unable to relax. He'd notified the sheriff's department of the litter on the road and had received reassurances that the matter would be taken care of. He'd also made arrangements for Liana's rental car to be driven back to the hotel.

He rubbed his bare chest and threw a discontented stare around the room. For once, there were no company fires he had to put out, no messages from frantic executives to be answered. Earlier in the day, he had even sent Margaret back to New York. He spied his briefcase sitting on the desk and thought of the papers it held. He was halfway across the room before he stopped himself. Generating work *wasn't* what he wanted to do tonight.

He grabbed a shirt from the wardrobe and slipped it on. Without bothering with the buttons, he headed out of his room and down the hall. He didn't have far to walk. At room thirty-three, he stopped. In a last-ditch effort to force reason on himself, he stared at the numbers.

Thirty-three. Thirty-three. Thirty-three.

Hell! This deliberation was doing no good. His mind was already made up and had been for some time.

A few moments after he knocked, Liana opened the door. From the looks of her, she had just come out of a bath. The hem of her teal-blue satin robe brushed her upper thigh. A matching ribbon held the pale blond mass of hair on top of her head. Silky baby tendrils curled along her hairline, the ends of the ribbon trailed to her shoulder. Her skin was flushed and glowing.

She appeared soft and sensual with a touching vulnerability. Every man's dream. And his very own personal nightmare. Heaven help him.

Without waiting for an invitation, he walked into the room. "I thought I should check on you."

"Why?" she asked, slightly breathless. She hadn't expected to see him again tonight, but now that he was here, so extraordinarily sexy in hip-molding black slacks and opened gray shirt, she knew she had hoped he would come. But this wasn't a good situation. Just by entering her room, he had charged the air with danger and excitement.

"Chalk it up to my being bored as hell. Or to the fact that you nearly died today, and I thought looking in on you might be the thing to do."

"That's nice of you, Richard, but not at all necessary." She saw his eyes lower to her breasts, and to her horror realized her nipples had hardened at the sight of him.

"Have you eaten?" he asked, a slight thickness entering his voice.

Nervously she tightened the belt of her robe, then immediately regretted the action. Her aroused state was even more apparent with the satin stretched across her breasts. She clamped down on her emotions. "I'm not hungry."

"I am, but not for food."

Warmth suffused her, and to her chagrin, color came up under her skin.

"Invite me to sit down, Liana."

The knowledge that he knew exactly how he was affecting her gave her yet another reason to dig in her heels and resist the temptation to do as he asked. "No."

He threw a glance over his shoulder at the big four-poster bed. "Then invite me into your bed."

She touched her forehead and found it damp. It was residual moisture from the shower, she assured herself, not perspiration. "I don't think so."

"Why not?"

"Nothing pleasant happens when we spend time together."

"Ah, now, Liana, I don't think that's quite true. Besides which, if it is true, I think it's time we try to change it."

His voice had soft, coaxing tones in it, and she felt her body inclining toward the sound and him. She straightened. "Why?"

"Because the memory of what we once had together is there between us."

She shook her head. "Richard—"

"I'm talking about what we shared in bed. Don't tell me you don't remember."

If only she could forget! Sometimes she was almost able to convince herself that her mind had played tricks on her and that nothing could possibly be that wonderful. When they had made love, they had rearranged the solar system.

"Sex is not the only memory between us," she said, her voice softer than she would have wished.

He lifted his hand and reached toward her. She automatically dodged, jerking her head back.

He smiled, waited a heartbeat, and took hold of one end of a satin ribbon. "But like the adults we are, we've put all that behind us, haven't we?"

He was probing, and she should tell him that naturally she had put their past behind her. But there had been so many lies, and suddenly she was incapable of telling him one more—for now at any rate.

"Let's make new memories," he said very softly, fingering the satiny texture of the ribbon. "Right now."

Her knees went weak, her throat dried.

He took a step back and waved his hand toward the bed. Without pushing, pulling, or forcing her in any way, and without any more words, he was asking her to come to bed with him. There were so many things she could do at this moment, and all of them flashed through her mind like a video-tape on fast forward. But in the end, she knew she would do only one thing.

As if mesmerized she crossed the room. He went with her, and when he sat down on the side of the bed, she did too.

He noted her wariness, yet deep in her eyes, there was also a glittering of need that told him she wanted him as much as he wanted her. Her breasts lifted and pushed against the satin with every nervous breath she took. Lord, he needed to proceed so carefully with her. But how could he? Desire wound in his gut, sending signals of urgency to every part of his body. He allowed seconds to pass until he felt in command again. "Tell me something, Liana."

She blinked with surprise. She had half expected him to grab her to him and pull her down onto the bed. "What is it you want to know?"

The phrasing of her response reminded him of another question, the one that had haunted him night and day since she had left him. *Why in the hell didn't you love me as I loved you?*

He closed down that dark, tortured part of his mind where the question resided before it could break free and reach his lips. "I want to know—do I hurt you when I touch you?"

She tried to swallow and felt an unfamiliar rawness. "Every single time," she whispered.

A look of genuine perplexity crossed his face. "How? I know I'm not always gentle, but—"

"Your touch burns right through my skin. Sometimes, hours after you've left, I can still feel the burning."

His expression changed, becoming understanding and satisfied. "Don't be anxious. We'll take it easy, let you get used to the touching a little at a time." He reached up and slowly drew the ribbon from her hair. A cloud of pale hair came tumbling down and settled around her shoulders. Combing his fingers through the silky strands, he whispered, "I promise you something. By the end of this night, you won't remember what it's like not to have my hands on you. And the burning will be so much a part of you, you'll miss it if it's not there."

For a moment, she knew real fear. "That sounds like a threat."

He wrapped his hand around her neck and slid his thumb up the center of her throat, then back down until it rested right over the larynx. Holding her gaze with his, he pressed slightly. "This is what I would do if I wanted to threaten you."

She felt a portion of her air cut off; astonishingly she wasn't afraid. She had to guess the reason was stubbornness on her part. She knew it couldn't be trust.

Several seconds passed, then he eased the pressure and made a small circle over the area with the thumb, waiting until the fear disappeared and the need returned. "All right?"

She nodded.

With a smile, he dropped his gaze to the full sweetness of her mouth, then returned to the incredible teal of her eyes. He slid his hand down the center of her body to the valley between her breasts, then inside the robe and covered one full luscious mound. "*This* is what I would do if I wanted to make love to you." His thumb flicked across the stiffened nipple, sending electrically charged sparks to all corners of her body. Leaning forward, he brushed a soft kiss across her mouth. "Guess which one I want to do."

A soft moan escaped from between her parted lips.

At the defenseless spot where he previously had applied the pressure, he bent his head and licked, tasting the sweetness of her skin, breathing deeply of her natural perfume. As if he'd ingested an intoxicant, he grew light-headed.

Pulling away, he gazed at her. "Answer me, Liana," he demanded gruffly. "Tell me which one I want to do."

She shuddered; her words came with great effort. "I know you hate me."

He pushed her robe off one shoulder, baring her breast to his hungry gaze. He was aching for her and going this slowly was killing him. But there were compensations, such as the sight of the tiny, delicate rose-colored nipple of her breast that seemed to be begging for his attention again. He took the nipple between his fingers and thumb and tugged. "Does that feel like hate?"

She quivered with pleasure and closed her eyes. "Richard . . ."

He tugged again. "Does it?"

A fog of desire had closed in around her. Her hands shot out to his shoulders to steady herself. "No, it feels like . . . like wonderful."

"Wonderful? I want it to feel like *burning.*" He pushed her back on the bed and her robe fell open. Her nakedness was nearly his undoing. Her slim, ivory body was all he had remembered and then more. And he was about to have her. "Tell me when it feels like burning, Liana." His mouth came down onto the same tortured, throbbing nipple.

The burning started, searing into her, taking all the air in her lungs and her common sense with it. Heaven help her, she thought. She loved him—this man with the steel gray eyes and the hardened heart. For now she didn't want to think about the past that had been or the regrets that would come. She wanted only, mindlessly, to feel.

Her fingers stroked up into his hair. "I need you inside me."

A growling sound came from deep in his throat and he skimmed his hand over the flat plane of her stomach, through the pale, blond curls, and into the sweet warmth of her. "You mean like that?" he asked hoarsely right before he deepened the kiss, thrusting his tongue into the depths of her mouth.

Without waiting for an answer, he began to stroke her with his fingers, finding the place that sent streams of fire spiraling into her. She feared for her sanity. She'd been deprived for so long, and now the pleasure was almost too intense to bear.

"Is this what you want?" he asked huskily. "Is this what you meant?"

Pressure built; heat wound tighter and tighter inside her. His fingers caressed and invaded, creating sensations that she could not describe. And all the while he murmured words of encouragement, although she really couldn't say what they were exactly. Suddenly her body jerked, then her back arched off the bed, and she cried out.

He continued the stroking, never once pausing, but he quickly shifted and pressed his mouth to her taut stomach. And a savage shudder racked him as, with his lips, he felt the contractions of her release within her womb.

When she subsided, he undressed, then lifted and settled her against the pillows. He stretched out beside her and gently brushed a haze of hair from her face. "You never answered my question. Did I give you what you wanted?"

She turned her head and looked at him. His whole body was taut; the power of his desire evident in his hard masculinity. For the first time she smiled. "No. I want *you* inside me." She trailed her hand across his thigh to close her hand around him.

Her action took him by surprise, and a surge of desire made him momentarily weak. He closed his eyes and dropped his head back onto the pillow.

She rotated onto her side and nuzzled his throat with her mouth. "It's been so long since I've felt you filling me until I couldn't take any more of you. It's a feeling of being whole and full and complete." She looked down at her hand, reveling in the feel and the power of him. She gently squeezed. "I want *you*, Richard. *You.*"

With a loud, ragged groan, he rolled quickly between her legs and rose up on his elbows to look down at her. The teal color of her eyes had darkened almost to black. Her lips were reddened and swollen. He lifted slightly so that he could view her breasts. Stiffened points rose from the swollen mounds. With great precision, he lowered his chest on top of hers until he had positioned his nipples against hers.

She gasped. "Richard, please . . ."

Her plea lanced straight into him and pierced the most primitive part of him. He'd thought of this moment for so long; he wanted to draw the lovemaking out, to savor each of the little sounds she made, each of her pleas. But his body was betraying him and soon he would be the one begging. Every muscle he possessed had tightened until he was gripped by an agony of passion from head to toe.

Flexing his hips, he pressed against the already pulsating feminine nub. Hot pleasure scored through her. She caught her breath, her mouth slightly open.

His jaw clenched at the sight, and he remembered the feel of her womb's contractions against his mouth. He felt as if he were dying. "I guess I'm going to have to give you what you want, aren't I?"

She wrapped her legs around his back and cupped his buttocks with her hands. "Yes, Richard. Yes."

He drew back, then surged into her with a hard, powerful thrust.

After so long. After so long. The refrain hammered in his brain.

Once positioned in her, he tried to pause, to clear his mind. But thought-shattering sensations made it impossible. Then she lifted her hips to take him deeper. What small intellect that had remained fled, and an elemental wildness took over. He plunged into her, fast, rhythmically, desperate to put out the fire in his gut.

Yet he wanted her with him every step of the way as he took them both into the inferno, and so from somewhere he found a control he hadn't known he possessed. He was determined to teach her a new definition of burning, and when she stiffened and cried out, he knew he had succeeded.

Then he let himself go, and much to his surprise, learned the definition for himself.

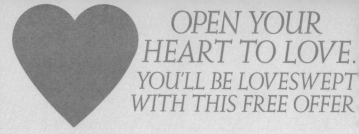

OPEN YOUR HEART TO LOVE.
YOU'LL BE LOVESWEPT WITH THIS FREE OFFER

HERE'S WHAT YOU GET:

1.
FREE! SIX NEW LOVESWEPT
NOVELS! You get 6 beautiful stories filled with
passion, romance, laughter, and tears...exciting
romances to stir the excitement of falling in love...
again and again.

2.
FREE! A BEAUTIFUL MAKEUP CASE
WITH A MIRROR THAT LIGHTS UP!
What could be more useful than
a makeup case with a mirror that
lights up*? Once you open the
tortoise-shell finish case, you have
a choice of brushes...for your lips,
your eyes, and your blushing
cheeks.
*(batteries not included)

3.
SAVE! MONEY-SAVING HOME
DELIVERY! Join the Loveswept at-home reader
service and we'll send you 6 new novels each month.
You always get 15 days to preview them before you
decide. Each book is yours for only $2.09 — a savings of
41¢ per book.

4.
BEAT THE CROWDS! You'll always receive
your Loveswept books before they are available in
bookstores. You'll be the first to thrill to these exciting
new stories.

**BE LOVESWEPT TODAY — JUST COMPLETE,
DETACH AND MAIL YOUR FREE-OFFER CARD.**

FREE-LIGHTED MAKEUP CASE!
FREE-6 LOVESWEPT NOVELS!

- ● NO OBLIGATION
- ● NO PURCHASE NECESSARY

(DETACH AND MAIL CARD TODAY.)

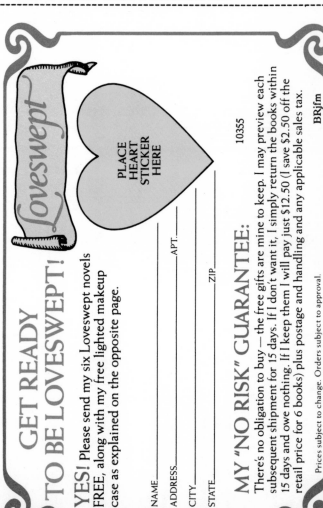

GET READY TO BE LOVESWEPT!

YES! Please send my six Loveswept novels FREE, along with my free lighted makeup case as explained on the opposite page.

NAME_____

ADDRESS_____ APT._____

CITY_____

STATE_____ ZIP_____

10355

MY "NO RISK" GUARANTEE:

There's no obligation to buy — the free gifts are mine to keep. I may preview each subsequent shipment for 15 days. If I don't want it, I simply return the books within 15 days and owe nothing. If I keep them I will pay just $12.50 (I save $2.50 off the retail price for 6 books) plus postage and handling and any applicable sales tax.

BRjfm

Prices subject to change. Orders subject to approval.

PLACE HEART STICKER HERE

REMEMBER!

- The free books and gift are mine to keep!
- There is no obligation!
- I may preview each shipment for 15 days!
- I can cancel anytime!

Six

Liana lay quietly, watching the draperies shift in the night breeze, pale and ghostlike. She was alone. Richard had made love to her twice, and then without a word, he had left.

But every aspect of the hours he had spent here in this bed with her was etched indelibly into her mind and heart. Their lovemaking had made all her memories pale. When they had come together tonight, the world had combusted and everything around them had gone up in flames. And they had been in the center of the conflagration, holding each other tightly, straining together, crying out their shared ecstasy.

Yet here she was alone.

It seemed she was destined to live with only memories.

Had she really been so stupid as to hope for something more? The answer came swiftly. Yes, she had. Without her being conscious of it, hope had begun to grow at the moment she realized she still loved him.

She admired what he had accomplished professionally. Her heart ached for the pain she knew she had made him suffer. Her desire for him knew no bounds. If he felt even a particle of what she felt . . .

No. To hope, even unconsciously, had been a mistake. She should have known better.

She squeezed her eyes shut, seeking resolve. If she had learned one thing over the years, it was that second-guessing her actions did no good, and in this instance, she had done enough rehashing.

She had to think with her head, not her heart.

She understood what had happened all those years ago in Paris; she didn't understand what had happened here tonight. But she accepted that nothing that had occurred between her and Richard, either in Paris or here at SwanSea, could be undone.

She knew he didn't love her. Maybe taking her to bed had been his own particular brand of revenge. Maybe now that he had his revenge, he would leave her alone.

She paused, realizing how dispassionate she sounded. She should be pleased, but she knew the truth. She might be eleven years older, eleven years wiser, but she was still as head over heels in love with Richard as she had been in Paris.

The sun would be rising in a few hours, and she had no idea what the day would bring. There was one thing she *did* know, however. Whatever happened, she did not regret tonight.

Richard lay sprawled across his bed. His sweat-soaked clothes were stuck to his skin; beneath his skin, pain ran like a raging river. A war was going on inside him, a war in which he was fighting himself. A war in which no matter the outcome, he couldn't win.

He swore aloud and rolled over onto his back. Nerve endings were screaming for him to rush back to Liana and bury himself in her as far as he could. But pride and an unyielding stubbornness kept him where he was. It was important to him that *he* had been the one to do the leaving tonight.

And after all, he told himself, he had had her. He didn't need her again.

He had already won one crucial battle—he had been able to force himself to pull away from the soft sweetness of her body and come back to this lonely room. True, every step he'd taken away from her had been like walking barefoot across broken glass, but the point was he had done it. If he went back to her now, it would be a defeat.

All he had to do was make it through the rest of the night without her, and then he would be all right.

There was just one thing: how in the hell was he supposed to do it?

And if somehow he managed to accomplish it, how would he get through tomorrow?

With a groan he rolled off the bed and went in search of his running shoes. A long, hard run until dawn would do the trick.

A premature darkness had come over SwanSea. Clouds that ranged in color from pewter to slate scudded across the sky, pushed by winds that carried the sure promise of a storm.

As Liana ran through the sculpture garden, the rose silk of her cape billowed out behind her, revealing the gray chiffon of the designer gown beneath.

"Double back, Liana," Clay called, snapping picture after picture. "Good, now go on to that next sculpture."

Off to the side, Richard watched broodingly as Liana stopped at a bronze form of Diana. The tall, leggy goddess had been sculpted with her garment flying out behind her as she paused midflight to look over her shoulder at a pursuer only she could see. Without being told, Liana emulated the goddess's pose. With her pearl gray gown and the rose cape swirling around her, Liana held the edges of the cape's hood and looked fearfully over her shoulder as if someone were chasing her.

This was the first time Richard had watched her work for any length of time, and he was struck by how demanding, both physically and mentally, her work was. He knew for a fact how little sleep she had gotten, yet there was no sign of how tired she had to be. She was able to strike the most difficult, awkward pose and make it look natural.

Amazing, he thought, recalling how hot and wildly responsive she had been the night before. Today she was as cool and as composed as the bronze statue she stood beside. She was exquisite in the long cape and gown, but last night, naked and flushed with passion, she had come to life and her beauty had transcended anything he had believed possible.

"Good, Liana, good," Clay said. "Now open the cape a little more so we can see the dress. Okay, lift the skirt slightly. More. More. Give me another angle, tilt your head. Good."

A pulse in Richard's temple throbbed. Clay's instructions to Liana were getting to him. Even if

the man was her photographer, he had no right
to order her around as he did. How could she
stand it? She seemed to have all the patience in
the world, whereas just the constant click and
whir of the cameras were irritating him, grating
against already raw nerves.

"Good," Clay called. "Now look this way."

She did and her gaze encountered Sarah, kneeling as usual beside Clay, watching her intently.
Sara smiled at her. For some reason, the act broke
Liana's concentration, and the mood and attitude
she had been adopting evaporated.

Clay cursed.

"Sorry," Liana said automatically.

Sara rose gracefully to her feet and walked over
to her. "It was my fault. You were just doing so
great, I couldn't help myself."

Liana's reply to the young girl lodged in her
throat as she looked over Sara's shoulder and saw
Richard for the first time.

"Liana? Forgive me?"

"Don't worry about it," she murmured.

"Get into your next gown, Liana," Clay said. "I
want to use this pre-storm atmosphere as long as
I can."

"In a minute."

"In a min—?" He broke off as he followed her
gaze to Richard. He frowned, then shrugged.
"Okay, go ahead. I need to check my film and
change cameras anyway. But *only* a minute. Sara,
Steve, let's talk about the next series of shots."

Richard crossed the distance that separated
them, took Liana's hand, and led her behind the
changing tent where they were out of sight from
the others.

Liana shivered. Violent, galvanic air surrounded

them, but the weather had nothing to do with the electric current that seemed to arc about Richard. He carried his own energy field, and faced with such a force, she could only wait.

He stared at her for a long moment with eyes as dark as the clouds above them. Finally he flicked the wide ribbons that tied the cape closed at her neck. "You look as if you just stepped out of a turn-of-the-century scene."

"That was the idea. A romantic look for a romantic setting."

"Romantic." He repeated the word thoughtfully. "You're certainly the right model for the job. Wearing that gown and cape, you have the perfect blend of femininity, fragility, and melting sensuality. But romance, Liana, is an ideal that doesn't exist."

"Maybe that's your belief," she said, hurt by his attitude, "but there are other people out there in the world who want very much to believe that beauty, adventure, and love—perhaps even chivalric love—exist, the kind you read about in storybooks. And if that belief is strong enough, who's to say that somewhere it doesn't exist?"

He gave a harsh laugh. "There's no such thing as love, Liana. You know that as well as I do. But beauty sure as hell exists. A man has only to look at you to know that. But it is what's beneath that beauty of yours that bothers me, and has for quite a while."

Despair gripped her; her love for him really was hopeless. "Was there something you wanted, Richard?"

His smile was quick and not a smile at all. "Of course. Last night should have told you that."

There had been no tenderness in his lovemaking, she reflected wearily. Why had she thought he might show her tenderness now? "Richard . . ."

"How much longer are you going to be doing this?" he asked abruptly.

"I don't know. That's up to Clay and the weather."

He scowled. "I don't mean today. I mean, how much longer is the whole shoot scheduled to last?"

"We've done just about half of the gowns."

"You'll be here until the end of the week?"

"Yes. The final shots won't be taken until the ball. The next day they'll auction off the gowns." She hesitated. "Why do you ask?"

"No particular reason. I was just curious."

The strange gray light of the approaching storm emphasized the fierce, angry expression of his face. She half turned away from him, finding it easier to look at the wildly churning sea. "How long do *you* plan to stay?"

"About the same length of time." He stared broodingly at her profile. The hood of the cape had blown off her head. The wind whipped at her hair and her skirts. Feathery streamers of her hair brushed at his face, the chiffon and silk of her skirts wrapped around his legs. Lightning flashed far out over the sea, a silver bolt momentarily connecting sky and sea. He saw her flinch in surprise. He took a handful of her hair in his fist, turned her, and brought his mouth down on hers in a plundering kiss.

The pleasure hit Liana immediately. Then the relief. He might not love her, but at least he wanted her.

She sagged against him and wrapped her arms around his neck. Clay's voice as he gave directions on the other side of the tent faded until she could hear only the soft, heated sounds that she herself was making.

Richard drew her closer, more relaxed now that she was in his arms. His tongue stroked hers with a hunger that vaguely astonished him. He couldn't remember ever kissing another woman the way he kissed Liana. Last night, there had been very few moments when he hadn't been kissing her—and there had been no part of her he had left untasted. He craved that same experience now, her taste, her feel.

Restless and needy, he moved his pelvis against her. *This wasn't going to be enough.* In fact, he felt as if he might come apart if he couldn't . . .

He slipped his hand inside the cape, down into the strapless dress, and wrapped his hand around her breast. As he did, he felt her shift slightly, making it easier for him to hold her. A hard shudder of satisfaction raced through his body. Her breast was made to fit in his hand. *His hand needed the touch of her.*

The smell of rain was in the air now. The smell of her was in his head. Lord, he had to have her!

Sara peeped around the corner of the changing tent. "Liana?"

Richard glanced over his shoulder. But he didn't release Liana, and he was unable to force himself to move his hand. His broad back shielded Liana, and all the girl would be able to see was that he had been kissing their star model.

"What is it?" he asked gruffly, all the while compulsively kneading Liana. She softly moaned, and he realized his arm around her was all that was keeping her upright. If they were only alone, he would sink with her to the ground, pull her skirts up out of the way, and take her there and then. Just the thought swamped him with heat. *"What the hell is it?"*

"Uh, we're moving the equipment out to the

bluff. Clay wants to try to get a picture of Liana there with the lightning behind her."

"I'll be there in a minute," Liana mumbled, willing to say anything to make Sara leave. Reality was slipping away from her.

"She said in a minute," Richard snapped to Sara and watched until she retreated.

Thumbing her nipple, Richard looked down at Liana. Her eyes were closed, her mouth slightly parted. Fresh desire surged through him. And fresh anger. "Why do you let that man order you around?"

Liana's lids slowly lifted. "Because he's in charge of this assignment. I work for him."

"I keep forgetting, don't I? How important your job and the money you earn is to you. Tell me, Liana. If I hired you to work for me and paid you twice, hell, three times what you're getting to do this job, would you do what *I* tell you?"

She swallowed, her attention torn between his words and his hand that continued to caress her breast and tease her nipple. "What you're talking about is making me a prostitute."

"That's *your* perception of my offer."

"Is it an offer?"

"Would you do what I tell you? Anything?"

"Not for money."

"What then?" he asked gruffly, pulling her closer against him. "Tell me. I'll find it, I'll buy it, I'll get it somehow."

You already have it, she wanted to say. *You have my love.* Instead, somehow, from somewhere, she summoned strength and jerked away from him.

He flexed the fingers of the hand that had just held her, then slowly rolled them into his palm until his hand was a fist. "Go back to work, Liana," he said in a low rough voice. "Do what Clay tells you to do. Earn more money. Give the world more of you. But no one will ever know you like I do. And no one will ever have you like I plan to have you."

Clay never got the picture he wanted on the bluff. Shortly after Richard stalked away, the storm hit. Drenched to her skin, Liana made her way back to her room and took a hot shower. Then she lit a fire in the fireplace, climbed naked into bed, and fell into a deep sleep. She awoke a few hours later and heard the rain pelting against the windowpanes. She got up and added more logs to the fire, then climbed back into bed and snuggled down into the covers. Warm and rested, she watched the shadows dance on the wall, thrown there by the light of the fire.

She didn't stir, not even when lightning lit the room and thunder rolled and boomed overhead, not even when the door to her room opened and Richard entered.

He closed the door behind him. "Your door was unlocked."

"Yes."

He engaged the lock, then walked to the bed. "Were you waiting for me?"

"Yes."

Slowly he began to undress. He unbuttoned his shirt, shrugged out of it, and let it fall to the floor. The fire's light immediately caressed his newly exposed skin, threading in and out of the mat of dark hair that covered his chest, and turning his shoulders and abdomen a warm bronze color. He stepped out of his shoes and reached for the waist-band of his slacks. His every movement sent muscles rippling beneath his skin, thrilling her.

The sheer maleness of him overwhelmed her. She itched to run her hands over the strong lines of him, to feel the heat of his body against hers, to inhale his clean masculine scent. When he pushed his slacks over his hips and down his legs, her mouth went dry. He wore no underwear; he was already fully aroused.

He slipped under the covers and took her into his arms. "Are you ready?"

"Yes."

He rose over her and cupped her buttocks with his hands, then with a thrust, buried himself in her. The possession was slow, hot, and greater than either of them had ever known before. But that was only the first time, and after that, they lost count. He stayed inside her all night long. Even when they were just resting, he never once separated from her.

They spoke very little. The pleasurable things they did to each other said everything. SwanSea sheltered them; the storm outside never touched them.

They had their own storm, a storm of passion and desire so intense, that daybreak found them in an exhausted slumber, arms and legs entwined, their bodies still fused together.

Liana heard the ringing of the phone through clouds of sleep, and at first she couldn't connect the sound with an action she should take.

Richard provided a clue. "Don't answer it," he said, his mouth somewhere near her ear.

Against her will, her mind began to work. "I should. It's probably Clay about today's shooting schedule."

He made a disgruntled sound and lazily flexed his hips against her. She felt him begin to grow deep within her, and she smiled softly. She pressed her lips against his throat and whispered, "If I don't answer it, he'll send someone to find out if there's something wrong."

With a muttered oath, he reached out a long arm to wrest the telephone from its cradle. The ringing stopped. Gazing down at her, he raised up on one elbow and pressed the receiver into the pillow. "Tell him you're going to be late this morning."

"Richard—"

He moved in and out of her, bringing her body awake and filling her with a liquid warmth.

"Tell him. All right?" he asked, continuing his lazy thrusting.

Her eyes beginning to glaze with passion, she nodded. He placed the receiver against her ear. Caught and held by the heat in his eyes, she murmured, "I'm going to be a little late this morning."

"Clay's not going to like that," an amused voice said.

Her mind instantly cleared. "Jean-Paul!"

Richard ceased all motion.

"I thought you were never going to answer the phone," Jean-Paul said. "Did I catch you in the shower?"

Richard pulled out of her, rolled to the other side of the bed, and threw his forearm over his eyes.

"Liana?"

"Yes, I'm here." A look at Richard's face told her he had retreated both physically and mentally from her. She felt empty and alone. She wanted to touch him, but she had the feeling that if she tried, his body would deflect her hand.

"Liana, you sound strange. Are you all right?"

"I'm fine, Jean-Paul. How are you?"

Richard surged off the bed and to his feet. "Could you hold on a minute, Jean-Paul?"

"Certainly, cherie. Unfortunately, I have nothing but time on my hands."

Richard rounded the bed and stepped into his slacks. She covered the mouthpiece of the phone with her hand. "Please stay, Richard. Don't go."

He yanked his zipper up and fastened the waistband of his pants. "I need fresh air. A lot of it."

"Richard—"

He jerked up his shirt from the floor and held it clenched in his fist. "If you're going to talk to him, Liana, I'm not staying."

"He's been sick," she said, trying to reason with him. "I want to find out how he's doing."

"That's very, very touching, but I'm out of here." He crossed the room and opened the door.

"Wait! I won't talk long. I promise."

The door slammed shut after him, and she sank back against the pillows. Her hand shook as she lifted the receiver to her ear. "I'm sorry to keep you waiting, Jean-Paul. I was in the shower."

"You never could lie worth a damn. You want to tell me about it?"

"No," she said, her sad gaze on the door. "No. Tell me how you are instead."

That night when Liana opened the door and Richard walked into the room, she wasn't surprised. She had come to realize that—no matter their past, no matter their present disagreements —as long as they were here at SwanSea, they would be lovers.

SwanSea was large; they could easily avoid each other if they chose. But the turbulent emotions and feelings they carried for each other easily converted to passion, and the power of their passion pushed against the walls of the great house, seeking release.

They could not be in this place without being together.

Now when she closed the door after him, the lovely, soothing room filled with tension. Richard's tension. He was wound tighter than a spring, and she knew why. *Jean-Paul.*

He came to a stop in front of the fireplace and gazed unseeingly at a stack of freshly laid logs. "I gather you finished your phone call?"

"Yes." She paused. "did you get the air you needed?"

"Yes."

"Richard, I'd like to explain about that phone call—"

He whirled around, his body taut, his expression fierce. *"No!* I don't want to hear one word about that phone call or the person who called you!"

"But—"

"I said *no,* Liana." He came to her and took her face in one big hand. He stared down at her for a long moment, and when he spoke again, his voice was softer, his manner calmer. "I don't even want to hear his name. All right?"

"I won't talk about the phone call if you don't wish. But, Richard, there is something else, something I've decided it's time you knew."

His thumb caressed her jawline, and his heated gaze focused on the fullness of her lips. "Does it have anything to do with tonight and what you want me to do to you when we go to bed?"

Her throat dried up as desire began low in her body. "No. It's about—"

His fingers tightened around her face, and his thumb brushed across her lips. "Then I don't want to hear it."

She wouldn't let him silence her. Not just yet at any rate. "I have to tell you this, Richard."

He slipped his thumb just inside her bottom lip to the soft moistness. "Maybe," he said huskily. "Maybe. But not tonight."

And then he replaced his thumb with his tongue.

Seven

Liana's sandals dangled from her fingertips as she made her way across the rock and driftwood-strewn beach the next afternoon. Perhaps because of the rocks, this beach was unoccupied, people choosing the sandier strip of land closer to the house. But Liana found the natural beauty and most especially the isolation of this beach to be exactly what she wanted, and she gave silent thanks that the day's shooting had gone well enough that Clay had called it quits early.

The late afternoon sun hung low in the sky and cast a golden hue over the glittering sand and glistening dark rocks. Foam-tipped breakers surged onto the sand and lapped at her bare feet. The sight, sound, and feel of the cold water soothed her. She had desperately needed this time of solitude and peace before she saw Richard again and a new storm began.

It had come to her quite suddenly last night that it was time Richard knew of the deceit she had perpetrated on him so many years ago. She had tried to tell him, but he hadn't been in a mood to listen, and it had taken only the persuasive powers of his hands and lips to distract her. But now after a day to think over her impulsive decision, she knew she was right.

She wasn't sure what she hoped to accomplish by telling him. All along she had felt it wouldn't make any difference if he knew. Even that time after her father's death when she had flown to New York with every intention of explaining, she hadn't held much hope that the truth would change things. She still didn't think it would. But seeing him again, being with him, realizing the depth of love she still held for him had convinced her that at the least he had a right to know.

She stopped to pick up a seashell, examined it briefly, then threw it back out to sea.

From his vantage point a short distance down the beach, Richard kept his gaze on her rather than the shell's flight. Long after the shell had disappeared beneath the waves, she stayed where she was, watching the sea. The wind lifted the hem of her loose-fitting sundress and braided itself through her long fall of hair; the dress and her hair were almost the same shade of pale gold. She looked solemn, beautiful, and very mysterious.

He would give up a major part of his possessions to know what she was thinking at this exact moment, he thought, then mentally cursed himself for being so stupid. He would never have the key to her. But at least, for this short time at SwanSea, he would have a part of her.

He walked up quietly behind her. "Were you testing your throwing arm, or was there something wrong with that shell?"

Her peace evaporated as soon as she heard his voice. Turning to face him, she reflected that she had given up asking how he was always able to find her when she could so easily elude everyone else. He seemed to have a built-in radar where she was concerned. "It was broken."

"And you're looking for one that's not?"

The question held only idle curiosity, she noted. Dressed in gray cotton twill slacks and a sky blue open-necked shirt, he appeared quite relaxed. Her need to believe that they could share an interlude of peace overruled her doubts. Tension slowly drained out of her. "Yes."

"Why?"

By unspoken agreement, they turned as one and began walking. "I wanted to take a shell home as a souvenir," she said. "The sea is so much a part of this place, it seems appropriate."

"I don't know if I agree. I think one of the gowns you've been modeling would be more appropriate. In fact, I'll buy you one."

She laughed lightly. "Thanks, but no thanks. A gown like one of those would only hang in my closet, gathering dust and taking up space."

"I've seen pictures of you at galas, Liana. I know you go out."

"When I attend functions where I will be photographed, designers lend me gowns to wear. It's free publicity for them."

Thinking about what she said, he paused to pick up a piece of driftwood, studied it for a moment, then drew back and hurled it out over the water. "All right then, I'll buy you one of the paintings that will be going up for auction in a few days. That would be better anyway, because I can guarantee that any of those paintings will appreciate in value."

She smiled, thinking of the simple cottage she called home. "Again, thank you, but I really wouldn't have a place to hang anything that valuable."

"Why not? You live in France, don't you?"

"That's right. In the country."

"A château?"

"Not even close." Still smiling, she nodded toward an outcropping of boulders. "Let's sit for a while."

With lithe grace, he levered himself to the highest point, where erosion and nature had joined forces to make a natural seating area, then he bent, clasped his hands around her waist, and easily lifted her to join him.

"All right," he said, after they were settled onto the sun-warmed rock, "tell me about your home."

She stretched out her legs in front of her and leaned back on her hands. "My house is very small, very old, and quite simple. But it has a great deal of charm and character, and I love it."

"But you have other homes, right? This country place isn't your only home."

She almost laughed, because he looked so puzzled. "I only need one home. When I'm on assignment, my contract stipulates that a place to stay be provided for me." He was silent for so long, she added, "The difference between the perception of my life and the reality is a chasm as large as the Grand Canyon."

Her remark drew his gaze, and his eyes were so clear, she felt she should be able to see all the way to his soul. But the clarity was deceptive, and unseen barriers blocked her way. "You don't believe me?" she asked, her tone deliberately light.

"I don't have any reason not to." He reached out and brushed back a wind-tossed strand of hair that had fallen across one ivory cheek. "You've changed my mind. I'll buy you jewelry. Maybe aquamarines, or even sapphires, whichever I can find that would come close to the color of your eyes."

She laughed. "Why do you have to buy me anything?"

"I don't *have* to. I *want* to."

Her laughter faded. "You don't owe me a payment of any type, Richard."

"No, you're right, I don't. But you wanted a souvenir, and I'm trying to think of something you'd like."

"I told you what I want. I want a seashell."

"Then I guess I'll have to help you find one."

A feeling warm as the sunshine that surrounded them slowly grew within her. "That would be nice. Thank you."

"You're welcome." His brow suddenly knit. "Now that I think about it, I can't remember ever seeing you wear any jewelry, either here or in photographs. Is there any particular reason why?"

"No, except again, jewelry doesn't really fit in with my lifestyle." She paused. "I own only one piece of jewelry, and I cherish it."

"Did Savion give it to you?"

The sudden tension in his voice cut into the tranquillity they had been sharing like a piece of jagged glass. She rushed to repair their peace. "Jean-Paul has never given me any jewelry."

"Then who?"

"An elderly lady I met in Paris about ten years ago. She was my next-door neighbor in the building where I took my first flat. She was bedridden and had a full-time nurse living with her, but from the moment I met her, we were friends."

"What did she give you?"

"A brooch in the shape of a lily. In fact, I've worn it since I've been here."

He nodded. "That's right, I remember now."

"Leonora—"

"Leonora?"

"That was her name. We got along wonderfully. I visited with her several times a week. My visits seemed to cheer her up. I don't think she had anyone else, but she told me stories of the man she had loved and their life together." Her eyes narrowed against the light dancing on the water. "She gave up everything for his love."

"Then she was a fool. There is no such thing as love."

She turned her head and met his gaze. "She thought differently. She told me she didn't mind dying, because she had known true happiness and love. Once she mentioned a regret, a major one apparently, but she never explained. She gave me the brooch right before she died."

"Why?"

"I don't know." She didn't want to tell him that Leonora had often said how much the sadness she saw in Liana reminded her of herself as a young woman. And of course she wouldn't tell him how Leonora had told her that one day she, too, would find true love. He would scoff, and she didn't blame him. Love was a subject better left undiscussed between them.

He threaded his fingers through her hair and tilted her head toward him. Then he kissed her, quite softly, quite gently.

"Would you settle for a piece of driftwood?" he murmured.

Bemused by the tenderness of his kiss, she wasn't sure she had heard him correctly. "What?"

"Driftwood. That is, if we can't find a suitable shell."

She smiled. "A piece of driftwood would be nice."

They scoured the beach, and in the end, chose

a piece of driftwood for him and a seashell for her. Later, as Liana showered and changed for dinner, she reflected that the afternoon had been a truly happy time, a time she would remember in the years to come as vividly as she recalled the nights of ecstasy they had spent here.

She met Richard downstairs in the dining room, where they enjoyed a long, leisurely dinner. He seemed totally relaxed, and she soaked up his attention. Every time he smiled at her or they shared a laugh, a secret sensation of pleasure tingled through her. But her happiness was moderated by what she knew was to come later—the story she had to tell him. As much as she hated to jar their current harmony in any way, that was just what she had to do.

When they returned to her room, Richard undressed, leaving on only his trousers, and stretched out on the bed. She undressed, too, and put on her robe, but she delayed going to bed. Instead, she wandered around the room, picking up something in one place, putting it down in another, trying to decide how she should begin. She wasn't aware that Richard was watching her until he spoke.

"What's wrong, Liana?"

She glanced over her shoulder at him. "Nothing."

"Then why are you way on the other side of the room? Why aren't you over here with me?"

She smiled briefly, thinking how much easier it would be to go to him, crawl into bed beside him, and give herself up to his incredible lovemaking. She actually took several steps toward him before she could stop herself.

She shook her head. "There's something I need to tell you."

"Later."

"I have a feeling that if I don't tell you now, I never will, and this is something you should hear."

His facial expression went from relaxed to tense in less than a second. "If it's about Savion, I don't want to know."

She walked to the end of the bed and wrapped an arm around one of the sea-green draped posters. "Actually this is about me and what a stupid, naive young woman I was at one time."

He shifted impatiently. "I don't see the point in rehashing the past, Liana."

"This isn't a rehashing, Richard. This will be information that is entirely new to you."

He rubbed his forehead. "I've lived all these years without knowing. I don't see why it's so important now."

An odd thought floated through her mind: he sounded as if he were afraid he would be hurt by what she wanted to tell him. "It's important to me, Richard," she said quietly.

He made a sound of exasperation. "All right, I give up. Let's get this over, whatever it is. Say what you have to say."

This wasn't beginning well, she reflected nervously, but then she hadn't really expected anything else. She ran the tip of her tongue over her lips. Both her throat and her lips felt dry. "I guess I should start with my father."

"Your father?" he said, surprised.

She nodded. "His name was Donald Gordon, and he owned a small textile business that he'd inherited. The name of that business was Gordon and Sons. The Gordon in the title was my grandfather, who founded the company, the Sons was my father."

She waited for Richard to show some sign of

recognition, but all he said was, "Why was your father's name different from yours?"

Her fingers fiddled with the diaphanous material that draped the bedpost. "I decided to take my mother's maiden name for professional purposes."

"So your real name is Liana Gordon?"

"That's right." She pushed away from the bed and slipped her hands into the pockets of her robe. "At any rate, apparently my father wasn't much of a businessman, although I didn't find that out until later. I was finishing high school about the time the business began to fail. Things went from bad to worse until it reached the point where everything rested on the company getting one contract." She paused. "Unfortunately for him, you were going after the same contract and you won."

Richard bolted straight up in bed. *"What?"*

She nodded. "It was the Rhiman Industries contract."

"I remember." He frowned. "That must have been about twelve years ago."

"That's right. My father told me you were young and hungry and had underbid him." Her throat tightened. "He also told me you were unscrupulous."

"What else did he tell you?" he asked in a soft, ominous voice.

"That the only reason you won was because you had cheated to get the contract. Then in the next breath, he told me that he had lost everything. Not too many days later he tried to commit suicide."

He came off the bed and strode to her side. "Good Lord, Liana, suicide?"

Her lips formed a sad smile. "Oh, he didn't succeed. He botched the job, and he was left an invalid." She tried to laugh but it ended up a sob.

"So there I was, just out of high school, no real job skills and a mountain of medical bills that grew bigger every day. I had one thing going for me."

"Your face."

"Yes."

He didn't move, but it seemed to her that he had physically withdrawn from her. "You already told me how you got to the Paris designers."

"And thank goodness that happened." She drew a deep breath. "I finished one job and started looking for another. I had made quite a few contacts while I was there, and I thought my chances would be better in Paris than back in the States. Then one day quite by accident, I read in the paper about a young American businessman who was brash enough to come to Paris and try to sell textiles to the French."

His grim expression told her he knew what was coming next, and this time he did move a few steps away from her.

She made a helpless gesture with her hands. "It was pure impulse on my part. To my everlasting regret, I didn't even stop to think things through. I went to your hotel and flirted with one of the young men who worked behind the desk until he found out your schedule for me. Then I arranged to be in the same place at the same time."

"Tell me something, Liana." His tone held a quiet, deadly quality. "How did you know? How did you know that I would take one look at you and fall like a ton of bricks for you?"

"I didn't. It's just that making you fall in love with me was the only way I could think of to hurt you. I had no money, I had no power—"

"You only had your beauty," he finished for her. "Your face, your body, your eyes, the way your skin smelled and tasted—" He broke off and turned away. "I don't want to hear any more."

She put her hand on his arm and tried to make him look at her. He wouldn't budge, and she had to circle him until she was in front of him.

"You have to listen to me."

"I don't *have* to do anything."

Tears sprang into her eyes. "Please. *Please*, Richard. Just listen for a few more minutes."

"Damn you, Liana!"

She lay her palms flat on his chest, feeling as though the contact would somehow help her get through to him. "I fell in love with you."

He gazed down at her, his expression blatantly incredulous. "How can you even say that?"

Tears slipped from her eyes and ran freely down her cheeks. "Because I did fall in love with you, although that obviously wasn't the plan. But, think about it, Richard. We couldn't have had the incredible two weeks we had if—"

He tore away from her. "What the hell difference does it all make now, Liana? That was a long time ago. It's *over*."

She dashed at the tears with a shaking hand. "Maybe it doesn't make a difference, but I want you to know the whole story."

"Why? To soothe your conscience? To absolve you of guilt?" His voice and hand sliced through the air like a knife. "Forget it, Liana. It's not my job to give absolution."

She couldn't stop her tears, nor could she stop before she'd told him everything. "Try to see it from my point of view. I had fallen in love with the man I believed had destroyed my father. To make matters worse, I had become involved with that man for the sole purpose of destroying him."

"By making me fall in love with you," he said with a flat sarcasm.

"That's right."

"Well, honey, you sure as hell made me fall in *something* with you, but it was more than likely lust, and you didn't come near destroying me."

"I'm glad."

He uttered a disgusted sound and dropped back onto the bed.

"Richard, I *had* to leave you."

"Right. And before you left, you just had to tell me that you didn't love me, in fact had never loved me."

"I told you that so you wouldn't try to stop me. Don't you see? I couldn't bring myself to tell you the truth. I felt trapped and needed to get out quickly. I couldn't go on living with the man who had destroyed my father, nor could I live with the idea of destroying you. But, Richard, don't doubt that I loved you."

"Love." He sneered as he infused the word *love* with contempt. "And of course, your love for me is why you went to Savion. Because you loved *me.* It all makes perfect sense, Liana." He crossed his hands behind his head and stared at the ceiling.

Bands of pain were binding her chest, drawing tighter and tighter, but she went on. "I was hurting, because of what I had done and because of what I thought you had done. I could see no resolution. Jean-Paul provided me with a safe haven. He expected nothing of me—"

His harsh laugh interrupted her.

What was the use, she thought in despair. He didn't want to hear any of this, and now she was sorry she had forced him to listen. She had opened sealed-over wounds and destroyed whatever tenuous relationship they had managed to achieve here at SwanSea.

"Are you finally through?" he asked.

"No," she said slowly. "There's one more thing. Six years ago, my father died, but right before he did, he confessed to me that he had used you as a scapegoat, as a cover for his own incompetence." She laced her fingers together and stared down at them. "You see, he couldn't accept the responsibility for his failure, and he couldn't bear for me to know that he had lost the company that he considered my birthright." For once, Richard didn't say anything; he was staring at the ceiling again. "As soon after the funeral as possible, I caught a plane to New York. I planned to tell you everything and beg your forgiveness. But when I called your office from the airport, I found that you were on your honeymoon. The news, coming right on the heels of my father's death, was devastating to me." Completely miserable, she shrugged. "That's it. You finally know everything."

She waited for a reaction, expecting an explosion of some sort, but his silence continued, stretching, growing, like an impenetrable wall.

"Richard?"

"Come to bed, Liana."

The quiet resignation she heard from him shocked her. "Is that all you have to say?"

He slowly moved his head on the pillow until he could see her, but his eyes appeared dead, without expression. "I'll admit that when you left me eleven years ago it seemed like a big deal. I took it hard. But looking back on that day, it was only my pride that was hurt, nothing more."

"But—"

"There is no love, Liana. Love is only a word people use as a rationalization for passion."

She couldn't think of a thing to say; she felt as if she'd been hit in the stomach.

"Come to bed," he said again.

The room began to spin, the floor tilted precariously. Somehow she made her way to the bed without falling and managed to lie down.

He didn't touch her. She didn't touch him.

She stared unseeingly into the darkness, listening to the quiet, even pattern of Richard's breathing, and the ear-piercing screams in her head.

And when she awoke, she was alone. Again.

The cloud-shrouded night provided little illumination. Richard used the beam of the borrowed flashlight to light his way along unfamiliar paths as he ran. And ran. And ran.

Damn Liana!

What had she expected? That she could tell him that incredibly stupid story and the past eleven years would be erased? The emptiness. The loneliness. The pain.

Or was telling him her way of inflicting even more pain?

Bitterness choked him until he thought he wouldn't be able to go on. But he continued running, through woods, across meadows, trying to exorcise the demon that tormented his soul—the woman who had somehow imbedded herself so deep inside him, he feared for his sanity.

Even if the first part of the story were true, even if she had set out to hurt him by making him fall in love with her because she thought he had cheated her father, why had she left him?

She said that she had fallen in love with him. He didn't believe it. He *couldn't* believe it. The hateful words she had uttered right before she had walked out the door were forever carved into his brain. "I don't love you," she had said. "I've only been playing with you." And then she had gone straight into the arms of Jean-Paul Savion.

Damn her straight to hell.

He ran, and he ran, and he ran.

And when he found himself in front of her door, he opened it, and went to her.

Through the gray light of dawn, he saw that she was awake.

"I think I hate you," he said quietly as he shoved his sweatpants down and thrust desperately into her.

She arched up to receive him, and his mind went blank, as a dark, burning desire took over.

And every time he drove into her, he repeated how much he hated her.

Eight

The sound of voices bounced off the rows of paint-ladened canvases, lifted to the high ceiling, and returned to fill the long gallery of SwanSea. Liana didn't hear.

Rosalyn, who was newly discharged from the hospital and who had insisted on resuming work, fussed with Liana's hair, trying to achieve the disordered look of the woman in the painting that hung high in the second tier of art on the wall. Liana didn't feel.

Sara tugged at the folds of the blue gown she had donned for this series of pictures. Liana didn't notice.

Steve shoved a light meter toward her face. She didn't flinch.

With great force of will, she had retreated to the place in her mind where their hands, their voices, their gazes didn't intrude. She had determined that she was through with hurting.

Briefly, foolishly, she had opened herself to Richard and, in the process, had allowed herself to become too vulnerable. No more.

Even the fact that Richard was among the spectators gathered around them didn't bother her overly much. She accepted his brooding presence, just as she accepted the fact that he would kiss and hold her again.

She didn't have the strength to refuse his lovemaking; there were times when she wanted him more than she wanted to live one more moment. But she had decided she could enjoy the interlude of their passion with relative safety if she kept her eyes on the rapidly approaching time when they would both leave SwanSea and go their separate ways. In a matter of days she would be alone again in her little house deep in the French countryside. She would be safe there. Until then, she had to protect herself.

"She needs flowers in her hair," Clay said, eyeing her critically.

Rosalyn bent down to a florist box on the floor. "I have them right here."

Sara draped an almost transparent blue stole around her shoulders; Rosalyn began to weave small cream-colored flowers through her hair. Liana endured their attentions patiently, understanding that their aim was to make her look as much like the young women of the art nouveau period as possible—the women with their flaring veils and streaming hair, who had posed for the posters and paintings of the period.

"The wind machine is ready," Steve said to Clay.

Clay looped a camera around his neck and made one last check of its settings. "Okay, now, Liana, I want you to stand on that ladder over there so that I can get both you and the painting in the frame. Can you do that?"

"Of course."

"Good." He patted her arm, then turned his

attention to his crew. "Time is getting critical, people. The climax of this shindig, the ball, is tomorrow night, and we've got an awful lot of work to do yet. We can't afford any more delays, so let's all give our best. Liana, the ladder. Steve, the wind machine. Sara and Rosalyn, get out of the way. Let's go."

Liana stepped onto the first rung of the ladder. As soon as the wind hit her, the feather-light fabric of her gown began to pulsate around her in sinuous swirls and undulations, and she set about to capture the sensual, languid mood of the first painting Clay had chosen to spotlight.

"Go higher," he called.

She stepped onto the next rung and the next. The sturdiness of the ladder allowed her to pose freely without the fear that it would tip over. Holding onto the top of the ladder, she arched backward so that her hair and dress flowed outward with the wind's current.

"Beautiful, beautiful," Clay murmured, snapping away.

She climbed higher, and when she'd gained the next to the highest rung, she released the top of the ladder and threw her hands upward.

The cracking sound barely intruded on her concentration, but then she felt herself begin to slip and she realized the rung she was standing on had broken.

The splitting wood halved and her feet dropped through to the next rung, but her high heels couldn't gain a purchase and she kept slipping. Just as she made a grab for the top of the ladder, her shinbone struck the edge of a crosspiece and pain lanced through her. Onlookers gasped their alarm, her dress ripped, and then she was falling backward to the floor.

When she opened her eyes, she saw a clearly enraged Richard kneeling over her.

"Don't move."

What was he mad about now, she wondered dimly, as Clay's face swam into her view, then Steve's. Both looked worried and concerned—completely different emotions from Richard's.

For some reason the whole thing struck her as funny, and she began to laugh. But the breath had been knocked out of her, and the laugh turned to a cough, then a sob, then a groan.

"Are you in pain, Liana?" Steve asked quickly. "Do you need a doctor?"

"I'm sure she does," Clay said. "Go call for one."

She felt Richard pick up her hand, his fingers stroking it gently. His voice, however, sounded like he had swallowed broken razor blades. "Where the hell did that ladder come from?"

"Right here," Clay said, throwing a strange look over his shoulder at Sara. "We borrowed it from the hotel. Sara went and got it this morning."

"That's right," the younger woman said.

Sara looked pale, Liana thought absently, as she came to stand over her.

"One of the maintenance people told me where the ladders were kept," Sara continued, her words rushing out in a nervous tempo. "I went before we started this morning and took the only one that was there."

"Didn't you look to see if there was anything wrong with it?" Richard asked her. It wasn't until Liana's soft gasp penetrated his agitation that he realized his grip had tightened on her hand. He eased his hold.

"No. I just assumed—"

"Well, you assumed wrong, didn't you?"

Clay's gaze had been going between Richard

and Sara, following their conversation. "For heaven sakes, forget the damned ladder. The important thing is Liana." He looked down at her. "How are you, honey?"

Her brief hysterical period had passed; a throbbing ache that seemed to encompass her entire body had set in. "I've been better." She tried to sit up, but grimaced when she felt sharp twinges in various parts of her body.

"Don't move," Clay and Richard said simultaneously.

"Trust me," she said dryly. "If I don't move now, I may never move." Her second attempt to sit up was a success.

Clay reached out a hand to support her back. "You may have broken something, Liana. We need to get you to a doctor."

This conversation sounded vaguely familiar, she thought dryly. She shook her hair out of her face, sending a dull pain through her head and flowers showering to the floor. "Nothing's broken. I've just managed to collect a few more bruises, that's all." She glanced at Richard. "Help me stand."

When he hesitated, she moved to stand by herself.

"Dammit, Liana," he said, reaching out to her.

Once she was on her feet, her knees buckled, but then braced to hold her weight. She fixed a determinedly bright expression on her face. "See? I'm fine."

Richard muttered a curse under her breath. "I'll take you up to your room."

"No, I'm going to continue working. Clay, which dress do you want me in next?"

Clay looked at her as if she had lost her mind. "What?"

She managed a grin. "Why are you so surprised?

You're the one who told us how much we have left to do and how little time we have left to do it."

"That was before—"

Richard's fingers closed around her upper arm. "Liana, quit being so stubborn and let me take you upstairs."

She pushed his hand away. "I'm here to work, Richard. I told you that right from the first day." She glanced toward Rosalyn, whose concern for her had made the blotches on her face more pronounced. The quickest way to wipe the anxious look off her face, Liana knew, was to give her some way to feel helpful. "Rosalyn, do you have any aspirin?"

Rosalyn snapped into action. "In the makeup bag. Come on, honey, I'll give you a couple and we'll get you into the next dress."

Clay eyed Sara for a moment, then shrugged. "Okay, people, let's set up for the next shot."

Steve and Sara set to work.

Richard strode down the long gallery toward the door, his brow knit in thought. There seemed to be a lot of bad luck on this shoot, and all of it was being experienced by Liana. It could be a coincidence. Then again . . .

Richard went to several maintenance people before he found the man with whom Sara had spoken. The man wore a uniform with the name Bill monogrammed over the chest pocket. Richard passed a hundred dollar bill to him to assure he would be the only one getting this man's information.

Bill pocketed the money with a smile. "We have more than one ladder, and as I recall, when the lady came to ask me where they were and if she could borrow one, all but two were in use."

"Two? Are you sure?"

Bill nodded. "Sure I'm sure. I told her to help herself."

"Were they both in good repair?"

Bill looked vaguely shocked. "Absolutely, Mr. Zagen. This is SwanSea. We wouldn't tolerate any broken ladders."

Liana gave a sigh of pure bliss as she sank into the steaming hot water of her bath and rested her head on the rim of the tub. She was exhausted and it felt as if every bone in her body hurt. But at least, she thought, she had the satisfaction of knowing she had managed to complete the day's shooting schedule.

The heat of the water penetrated through to her bones, and slowly her knotted muscles began to loosen. Her mind drifted, and against her will, her thoughts returned to the moment when she had heard the crack of the rung as it broke in two. How was it that the topmost one had broken when the others hadn't? The wood must have been rotten or weak or . . .

She remembered how Steve had come to her after she had fallen down the grand staircase. He had intimated that the light might have been rigged.

Despite the heated water, she suddenly shivered. The thought that someone might actually be trying to hurt her was incomprehensible. She had discarded the idea once before and she did so again. She didn't have an enemy in the world.

Unless she counted Richard. She discounted that idea as quickly as it had come to her. Richard certainly made a formidable enemy, but causing her physical harm wasn't his style. He might

cut her to pieces with slashing words, but he
never left any visible scars. And he might give her
sexual pleasure so intense she sometimes feared
she would die. But after he was through making
love to her, she fell into a deep sleep, not into
death.

But what if someone else . . .

She heard the outside hall door to her bedroom
open and knew it was Richard. Her first impulse
was to speak to him about her doubts, but the
impulse was immediately squelched.

She felt threatened and a little frightened, but
Richard was the last person to whom she could
show any weakness. He had the power to hurt
her, the kind of hurt that wouldn't kill or bruise,
but would go much deeper and cause irreparable
harm.

When he appeared in the doorway, she smiled.
"Hello."

He leaned his shoulder against the doorframe
and crossed one ankle over the other. Staring at
her, he felt the familiar stirrings of desire, the
powerful, blood-boiling kind that only she could
make him feel.

Tonight yet another satin ribbon tied her hair
atop her head, this one blue, and its ends min-
gled with her wheat-colored curls. His gaze dropped
below the clear bath water to her breasts and
their taut rosy peaks. In two steps, he could have
one of them in his mouth, he thought, and Lord
knew he needed the succor he would receive.

He forced himself to look at something else. The
triangle of pale hair low on her body drew his
attention, and then her legs. Just looking at those
long, lovely legs and remembering how they felt
around him made his gut clench. Every inch of
her skin that he could see had a pearlescent sheen

to it, and a fragrance, vaguely floral, vaguely haunting, rose from the water and permeated the air. If he didn't do something and quick, he would lose himself in her for the rest of the night.

"Do you always leave your door unlocked?"

The serrated edge of his voice caused her to throw him a wary glance. "Not always."

"You did early this morning. I came back from running and was able to walk right in."

"As I recall, I didn't know you had left." She reached for the soap and washcloth. "I woke up right before you returned."

He remembered. He had been in agony and had desperately needed to assuage that agony in her sweet, firm body. Just as he wanted to do now. His jaw tightened. "What about tonight? Anyone could have walked in."

"But anyone didn't," she said, unwilling to tell him that she had left the door unlocked for him. "You did."

"That lock is there for a reason, Liana. Use it."

She skimmed the soaped cloth down one arm and across her chest. "Is there any particular reason why we are talking about whether or not I lock my door?"

His eyes automatically followed the path of the washcloth, but his mind worked on how he would answer her. He had to be careful. If he were wrong about this half-formed theory that someone was trying to harm her, he could end up looking like a fool. And his number-one priority at the moment was to come out of this affair with her, unscathed and with his dignity and heart intact.

He rolled his shoulders in a nonchalant manner. "I just think that locking your door would be a sensible thing to do. Several unexpected things *have* happened to you lately." His heart picked up a beat as she lathered soap over her breasts. "You know, it's funny. When we were together in Paris, I don't remember you being particularly accident-prone. Of course, that could be because you spent a great deal of time on your back."

She hurled the dripping wet washcloth at him and had the satisfaction of seeing it land with a smack against his face.

It dispersed a portion of the tension he had been feeling. Smiling, he peeled it off him. "I guess you thought I deserved that."

"I guess I did."

His smile grew bigger, and he tossed the cloth back into the tub, where it landed in the water near one drawn-up knee with a plunk. "Okay, maybe I did."

She sighed. "Just say whatever it is you're trying to say, Richard."

He moved away from the doorframe and came to perch on the rim of the tub. Gazing down, he dipped his fingers into the water and absently made figure eights. "You've had three accidents since you've been here. I can see one, maybe even two—the fact that the road was littered with debris wasn't your fault—but three just seems a little excessive. And if you consider the face powder . . ."

Disturbed, she shifted position in the water. She had no way of knowing if he were simply talking to have something to say, or if he might be genuinely concerned. If she thought for one minute that he was concerned . . . She shut her eyes. *What was she thinking?* And why did she keep having to learn the same lessons over and over again. She might love him with all her heart, but he certainly didn't love her. And if by chance he did hold any concern for her, it was on a strictly superficial level.

"Liana?"

She looked at him again. "I'm clumsy. Things happen."

She was clumsy, he thought, like a bull was dainty. "If you had broken a leg or an arm or a neck today, what would have happened to the shoot?"

That was a question she had already asked herself, but the answer had given her no help as to what might be going on. "Nothing. They would have brought in another model and the shoot would have been completed."

He frowned. "So no one would benefit."

"No." She tilted her head and studied him. To be making idle conversation, he was asking awfully specific questions. She couldn't resist probing, but for her own protection she coated her words with a slightly mocking tone. "You sound worried about me, Richard."

Immediately he went on the defensive. "I wouldn't call it worry, more like curiosity. Sometimes it gets the better of me."

She sank into the water until it came to her chin. "Its hard for me to believe that anything or anyone could get the better of you."

His lips formed a hard smile. "That's the way I like to keep it." He reached beneath the water and scooped up the washcloth. "I bet you're sore," he said, skimming the cloth from her knee, up her thigh, and back again.

She blinked at the sudden change of subject. "A little."

"A lot, I'm sure. That was a hard fall you took."

"The hot water's helping."

He put his hand under her calf and lifted it so that he could better see the dark purple bruise that had formed on her shin. His eyes cut to her, his eyebrows arched.

She shrugged. "It doesn't hurt much."

He released her leg without comment and came to his feet. "How much longer are you going to be in here?"

All of a sudden she felt naked, in more ways than one. His strange moods had kept her almost continuously off balance since they had met again here at SwanSea. Tonight she was tired, bruised, and uneasy. She wanted to shield herself in some way, even if it was only with a thin layer of clothes. "I'm through," she said and stood.

Water sluiced down her body, sheening her with a luster he found hard to resist. Looking at her, he felt himself harden, but no matter what she said to the contrary, the fall had to have hurt her, and afterward, she had gone on to work ten straight hours. He would have to be a blind man not to see the exhaustion in her eyes.

When she stepped onto the bath mat, he reached for a large thick towel and wrapped it around her, then tucked the end of the towel between her breasts. It took him several moments to realize that his fingers were lingering.

Disturbed, he quickly pulled his hand away. She was too easy to touch, too easy to want. He needed to watch himself more carefully.

"Thanks," she murmured and brushed past him into the bedroom. There she went directly to the bureau inlaid with marquetry work that was set against one wall. From a drawer, she retrieved a candleglow-colored chemise and a matching pair of panties and slipped them on. When she turned to Richard, she found him already in bed, wearing only a pair of black briefs.

Excitement began to pound through her at the thought of the lovemaking that would come, and she realized how foolish she'd been to put anything on. While it was true she felt a little achy and more than a little vulnerable, she knew from past experience that when he took her in his arms, everything would go away except need of him. She crossed the room, slipped into bed beside him, and nestled against him with an unconscious naturalness.

He put his arm around her and drew her closer against him. "You smell like a secret flower garden," he whispered huskily against her hair.

"Secret?" she asked lightly, happier now that he was holding her.

He paused, wondering why he had used that word. Then an image came into his head of her in a breathtakingly lovely garden. She was the flowers, and the flowers were her, and he was the only one who knew her different fragrances. The strange and uncharacteristic image shook him badly.

"Wonderful," he amended. "You smell wonderful. You know," he went on, adopting her light tone with difficulty, "someone might make a fortune if they could bottle the scent of your skin."

She shifted the position of her head on his shoulder so that she could see him better. "I hate to tell you this, but the bath oil I use is available over the counter."

"Maybe what you put in your bath water can be purchased over the counter, but the way the chemistry of your skin reacts to it is unique." He hesitated as a thought occurred to him. "Do you have a flower garden at your house in France?"

"Yes." Now what were they talking about, she wondered, baffled. And why?

He lightly ran his fingers up and down her arm. "Tell me about your house."

"I already have."

"No, I mean *really* tell me about it. What are the

rooms like? How have you furnished it?" He needed to be able to think of her there in the years ahead.

She was confused. Why was he here in bed with her if he didn't want to make love to her? The only other time they had been in bed together without making love was last night, but that had been because she had told him about her father's deception and how it had affected their lives. She understood why he wouldn't want to make love to her after hearing that. But why not now? Unless . . . Unless he was being considerate of her because of her fall.

"Liana?"

"I'm here."

He chuckled, and his hand briefly squeezed her arm. "That's good. So are you going to tell me about your house?"

"Well, there's not a lot to tell. I've furnished it with pieces I've found over the years, pieces of no particular style, but that fit together beautifully because they're simple and comfortable. And I have white lace curtains hanging at the windows. I enjoy the way they look when the windows are open and the breeze catches them." As she talked, she relaxed little by little, until her eyelids grew heavy and drifted shut. "There's a big stone fireplace in the parlor, and in the winter I keep a fire going there. I love cold, rainy afternoons, because that's when I pull a chair up to the fire and read. I love mysteries."

She grew sleepy and her words slowed and softened. "My kitchen is big—cool in the summer, warm in the winter. One of my favorite things to do in the winter is to make a big pot of stew, the kind that takes two days to make, the kind you keep adding ingredients to. . . . And every plate I have is different from the other."

He heard her trail off as she gave herself up to sleep. The corners of his mouth lifted slightly. A good night's sleep was just what she needed. She'd been under quite a strain this past week or so, what with her work and those damnable accidents. And he was sure his presence on the scene hadn't helped the state of her nerves any.

He adjusted his position so that she rested more comfortably against him. The sound of her soft, even breathing acted as a tranquilizer. In the distance, the eternal surge of the ocean provided a calming white noise. Now that she was asleep, he reflected, he could go to his own room. . . .

He found himself staying. He didn't know why, but he felt a strange sort of contentment. Here in the night, holding Liana, there were no business pressures, no noises that jarred, no need to seek revenge. It was nice. More than nice, actually.

Too bad this contentment wouldn't last. He was scheduled to return to New York in a few days. All too soon the hostilities and struggles that layered a normal business day would resume. A frown creased his face. He supposed Liana would continue with her life, too. Did she have another modeling assignment lined up, he wondered, or would she return to her little house in France?

He stiffened as a thought occurred to him. Would there be more accidents when she left here? Maybe with even more dire results? He wouldn't be there to protect her. His frown deepened. Not that he had been able to protect her here.

But why would someone want to hurt her?

He gazed down at her again. Even in the half light provided by the moon, he could see how thin and fragile she was. Her weight hardly made an impression on him. How could anyone deliberately set out to hurt her? He paused as he had a new thought. Wasn't that what he had set out to do? But then that was different, he assured himself. The thought of actual physical harm coming to her made him sick to his stomach.

He pressed his head back into the pillow and closed his eyes. *Dammit.* What was happening here? And why did he care so much?

Richard wasn't sure when he finally fell asleep, just as he wasn't sure what time it was when he was awakened by the feel of Liana's hands on him. She was caressing him with a touch that took him from sleep to wakefulness in seconds.

Her lips brushed across his chest to his nipple, and he stiffened when her tongue flicked the tiny bud. "Liana . . ." He gasped. "What are you doing?"

Her palm slid down his body, and she took him in her hand. "I want you," she whispered. "Do you mind?"

He groaned, then gritted his teeth as her hand began to rhythmically stroke him and her soft lips skimmed to his other nipple. The sensations were electric, exquisite, overwhelming. She was possessing him, applying just the right amount of pressure at exactly the right moment and place. His head went back into the pillow, and his back arched as his mind tried to deal with what was happening to him. Other women might have done the same thing, but none of them had ever come close to making him feel this searing, heart-pounding pleasure. *Lord.*

He pulled her on top of him, and without guidance, she slipped onto him. His body jerked at the instant, scorching-hot jolt of excitement her act gave him.

She was moaning now as she flexed and circled

her hips against him. The fever that gripped his body moved to his brain. Through slitted eyes and the dim light, he could see her pale hair around her head and shoulders. Her breasts, full, taut, and tempting swayed with her movements. He reached up and grasped them; the feel of their weight and satiny texture in his hands nearly took him over the edge. He lifted his head to hungrily suck one rigid nipple into his mouth, and the fire leaped higher in his gut.

"Liana," he said on a long drawn out breath, and his head fell back to the pillow. He was going wild with frustration and need. She was in control, and he found he loved it.

Her rhythm became faster. He arched up to her, time and time again, but she couldn't seem to get enough. She urged him on with whispered words and soft erotic sounds, inciting him to meet her demands.

Every breath he drew hurt, and there was an unbearable pressure in him that screamed to be released. Gripping her hips, he drove upward, using all the strength he had. With a distant part of his mind, he heard her cry out, then he, too, was crying out. Shuddering convulsively, he heard his cries go on and on, then waves of fulfillment began to break over him—too potent to be endured, too powerful to live without.

Nine

Liana stretched lazily, bathed by the early morning sunshine that fell across the bed. When her arm brushed against Richard, she turned her head to look at him. He was still asleep.

Her heart filled to overflowing as she remembered what had happened between them just a few hours ago. Oh, she knew for him the preceding hours had been nothing more than just very good sex; but what he didn't know, would never know, was that she couldn't have made love to him so unreservedly if she didn't love him.

She remembered how in the middle of the night she had awakened clasped in his arms, and with her guard still lowered from her sleep, she had followed a natural urge. What had happened then had been unbelievable, and she would never forget it as long as she lived.

And in spite of their rigorous activities, she felt completely rested.

Following another impulse, she leaned over and planted a gentle kiss at the corner of his mouth.

He opened his eyes; the softness in his gaze delighted her.

"Good morning," she murmured with a smile. "'How do you feel?"

He lay his palm flat on her stomach and spread his fingers so that he was touching as much of her skin as possible. "I think the question should be, how do you feel?"

She stretched again, her hands above her head, her back arched, her breasts thrusting upward. "I feel *wonderful!*"

Without moving his hand, he stroked his thumb back and forth across the smooth, tender skin of her stomach. "Are you sore?"

"Only slightly," she said, relaxed again, but with her arms still above her head, "and since it came from such a pleasant activity, I don't mind at all."

The gray of his eyes darkened. Her breasts were inviting, perfect mounds, and so near to his mouth. It had been his intent to leave her alone this morning, but temptation overcame him. He bent his head and drew a waiting nipple into his mouth. *Lord.* What a fantastic way to start a day off! Her body gave him both energy and nourishment. Yet there was a problem, he reminded himself. No matter how hard he tried, he couldn't seem to get enough of her.

Last night, he had found something erotic and unbearably exciting about her being in control. But with the cold light of day came the reminder that he didn't like the helpless feeling his need for her gave him.

Her soft moan quickened his pulse, but he did his best to fight back the desire. He had to stop now, or he wouldn't be able to. Their lovemaking in the middle of the night had left him unnerved, and he needed time away from her to rebuild his defenses.

One final time, he drew on her breast. Then one more time.

"That was nice," she murmured a bit breathlessly, when he finally lifted his head. "Why did you stop?"

Wanting her as much as he did, her willingness for him to continue almost undid him. "Don't you have to get up?" he asked brusquely. "I mean, isn't Clay expecting you to be downstairs for the day's shoot?"

She ran her fingers lightly along his jaw and felt the roughness of his morning beard. "Not until later."

His head whipped back. "If I don't keep away from you, I'll give you whisker burns."

"I wouldn't mind."

"Dammit, Liana, your skin will be too red to be photographed." He was grasping at straws and he knew it.

Before, she might have let his irritation stop her. But last night had given her a new courage when it came to their lovemaking, and, she reasoned, the more memories she had to store away, the easier the long years ahead would be for her. "Haven't you ever heard of makeup?" she asked softly.

"Liana—"

"Please, Richard. I want you again."

With a harsh groan, he succumbed. "Then get ready, because you're going to need a ton of makeup—and not just on your face."

They made love, frantically, passionately, and later took a long, lingering shower together. And in spite of it all, they dressed in plenty of time for them to have breakfast.

• • •

Liana held Richard's arm as they descended the grand staircase and felt as though she were encompassed in a haze of passion and happiness.

Richard leaned over and whispered, "It's a good thing the shower water turned cold. Otherwise, Clay most certainly would have sent someone to find you, and when they came, you would have been as shriveled as a prune."

"But I'd be a happy prune."

In spite of the people milling in the hallway below them, he drew her to a stop on the next to the last stair and shook his head with wonder. "You're insatiable."

"Are you complaining?" she asked lightly.

"I love it," he murmured, his tone hoarse and thick. "I've already shown you how much I love it twice this morning, and if you'll say the word, I'll take you back upstairs and show you several more times."

A spike of heat lanced through her. "I wish we could, but I have to work."

He remained silent. When was he going to get enough of her? Stop wanting her? Stop needing her? And most of all, how was he going to be able to let her walk out of his life tomorrow?

She shook her head regretfully, seeming to follow his train of thought. "Today's our last day. Tonight's the ball."

He tensed. "Are you telling me you won't have any time to give me today or this evening?"

"That's not what I'm saying at all. I'm positive we'll knock off earlier than usual this afternoon, and the ball doesn't start until nine. In the meantime, though, I do need to work."

"Forget the work."

She looked at him oddly. He actually sounded

as if he couldn't stand the thought of them being apart today. "We couldn't do anything together, anyway, Richard. You'll be busy with the art auction. That's why you came, remember?"

"I remember exactly why I came," he snapped, then stopped before he made a fool of himself. What was wrong with him? He actually sounded petulant because she wouldn't spend the day with him. To make matters worse, his body was already starving for her again. He *had* to get a grip on his emotions; being apart from her would be the best thing for him. Maybe he wouldn't even see her again before he left tomorrow.

But there were the accidents. He hadn't forgotten the possibility that someone was trying to harm her—or worse.

"Then you understand—"

He held up his hand. "Enough. You've convinced me."

She laughed. "Well, darn."

"You *wanted* me to talk you out of working?"

"No." She slipped her arms around his waist and looked up at him with an unconsciously provocative smile. "But I liked that you were trying to."

He groaned, half-serious, half-goodnatured. "All I've got to say is that you're lucky we're surrounded by people."

"Why? What would you do?"

"Believe me, my mind is churning with ideas."

She laughed again.

"There's just one thing, Liana. Be careful today. Make sure anything you stand on is solid and well built. Don't even drink anything unless you see someone else pour a glass from the same container and drink it. Also, be extra careful about your makeup."

She gazed searchingly at him. "You're worried about me?"

His grin was meant to disarm. "I just don't want any more scars on that lovely body of yours. When I see bruises, I feel as if I have to handle you carefully."

His easy manner relaxed her. She grinned back. "Oh, really? I hadn't noticed you handling me with any particular care. As a matter of fact, I distinctly remember—"

He leaned down and kissed her quiet. When he finished, she forgot what they had been talking about. "We better get to the dining room," she murmured, "or we're going to cause a scandal right here on the stairway."

He laughed, turning her so that they could take the final steps to the immense entry hall. "I'm sure SwanSea's walls have seen much more scandalous events."

"You're probably right," she said, then noticed Caitlin speaking with a group of people. Her wave produced a smile and a friendly nod of acknowledgment from Caitlin.

"Caitlin will be running six different ways today in preparation for tonight's ball," she said as they threaded their way around yet another group. SwanSea was at capacity.

"And don't forget the auction. Speaking of which, are you sure you won't let me buy you one of the paintings?"

"I'm sure. I told you—"

Richard stopped, his expression instantly hostile.

Curious, Liana followed his gaze. Jean-Paul Savion was walking toward them.

Her mouth fell open; she'd thought he was still ill and at his home in Paris.

But she wasn't the only woman in the hall who stared.

Dressed as always in his trademark black, Jean-Paul was a tall man, with heavy-lidded dark eyes and long black hair, pulled back and secured at the nape of his neck. SwanSea was filled with celebrities for the weekend, but Jean-Paul had a presence that tended to halt women in their tracks.

When he reached them, he leaned down to her and kissed first one cheek, then the other. "Hello, cherie. Surprised?"

"Stunned, frankly. I thought you were too ill to travel."

"As you can see, I have recovered."

Actually, he didn't look at all recovered, she thought, but had no chance to say so.

He turned to Richard and raised his eyebrows in a manner both imperious and inquiring.

She couldn't imagine a worse time for this particular meeting to happen, she thought. But then again, she would be hard-pressed to come up with a good time. She tried to steel herself as best she could for what was to come. "Jean-Paul, this is Richard Zagen. Richard, Jean-Paul Savion."

Neither man made a move to shake hands, and each regarded the other with blatant antagonism and contempt.

Richard was the first to speak. "If you two will excuse me, I have a full day ahead of me."

She grabbed his arm. "But I thought we were going to have breakfast."

Richard pointedly fixed his gaze on Jean-Paul. "All at once, I've lost my appetite." And without another word, he whirled and stalked off.

Liana stared after him, unaware that her heart was in her eyes.

Jean-Paul regained her attention by taking her

hand and tucking it into the crook of his arm. "I, personally, could eat a horse. Do you suppose, Liana, that they serve horse here?"

She gave a sigh, inaudible to all but the man beside her. "I'm sure all you have to do is ask, Jean-Paul."

She signaled to the hovering waiter, then leaned back in her chair as he whisked her plate away. "All right, Jean-Paul. I've eaten. You've eaten. You've given me your latest medical report. You've told me about your flight over on the Concorde, about the young girl you met and you think might be interesting to photograph. You've even told me about the small plane you rented to fly you from New York to here. Now, don't you think it's about time you tell me why you're here?"

He tossed his napkin onto the table and reached into the pocket of his black jacket for a long, slim cheroot and a gold lighter. Only after he had lit the cheroot and replaced the lighter did he answer her. "I am here because of you, cherie."

"Me? I don't understand."

"Steve placed a call to me after you fell down the grand staircase. He seemed to think that the light could have been rigged to fall."

She rolled her shoulders uneasily. "I know. He told me, but the idea seemed so preposterous—"

"I thought so, too. I thought so, that is, until he called me and told me about Rosalyn's unfortunate reaction to the face powder. Except for a fluke, cherie, that powder would have been applied to your face."

"It was a strange allergic reaction. Chances are, if she had put it on my face, nothing would have happened."

He drew deeply on the cheroot, then exhaled a long stream of smoke. "Maybe you are right, maybe you are not. My guess is you are not."

She twisted in her seat. She should have been comforted by the fact that Jean-Paul was here and now she had someone to whom she could tell her fears. But she could only think about how furious Richard had been when he had seen Jean-Paul.

"It was Steve's call yesterday," he went on, "informing me of your fall from the ladder, that finally sent me to DeGaulle to catch the first available Concorde to the United States."

"Steve shouldn't have—"

"Steve did absolutely the right thing. The only thing that would have been better is if you, Liana, had called me yourself."

She fell silent.

Through a veil of smoke, he studied her. "I have never seen you more radiant," he said carefully. "I really hope you are going to tell me that Richard Zagan is not the cause."

"I'm afraid he is."

"Mon Dieu! Has he been here the whole time?"

She nodded. "At first the tension between us was thick enough to cut with a knife. Then," she shrugged, "things just exploded."

"Exploded." His face twisted with anger, and he savagely put out the cheroot in a crystal ashtray. "The question is—are you going to get caught in the fallout?"

She met his gaze levelly. "Without a doubt."

"Then put an end to it, Liana. Put an end to it right now."

"It will end on its own soon enough."

He took in the set features of her face and sighed.

"Then I guess while you are still radiant, I should photograph you."

"You're not going to take the shoot over from Clay are you? Not when we're so close to being finished."

"No, I'm not here to take over. But I *will* observe the final shoot today."

She shook her head. "You can't. It will shake Clay's confidence."

He leaned forward and jabbed the table with a finger. "Who the hell *cares* about Clay's confidence? What is important is that you remain safe."

"You can't do it, Jean-Paul. You know you can't. It wouldn't bother you one iota if another photographer watched over your shoulder. But then there are only a handful of photographers in the world as good as you. Clay will come apart if he thinks you're checking up on him."

"I *trained* him, Liana. He has had me present in the studio many times before."

"This is different. You trusted him enough to let him take this important assignment on his own, and he's done a very good job. Let him finish it."

"Merde!" Jean-Paul flung himself back against the chair.

She looked at him. "You know I'm right in this."

He held up a hand. "All right, all right. Maybe my presence will be enough to deter any more *accidents*. But, Liana, if I hear that so much as a hair on your head is harmed today, I will shut down not only the shoot, but this entire place."

His concern drew a smile from her, her first since she had seen him. "You look tired. Why don't you go up to your room and lie down?"

He rubbed his hand across his eyes. "I hate to

admit it, but I think I'll have to do exactly that. This virus hasn't completely left my system yet."

She stood, walked around the table, and kissed his cheek. "Get some rest. I'll see you this evening."

The dark clouds that gathered on the horizon during the afternoon set the mood for Clay, Liana, and the rest of the crew, and when the thunder, lightning, and rain came, the stormy atmosphere seemed right.

Even though Jean-Paul was as good as his word and did not show up at the conservatory where they were shooting, the knowledge that he had arrived was enough to affect everyone. Clay's nerves were evident in every order he gave, and his tension spread to the rest of the crew.

As for herself, Liana's strain increased by the minute. Richard's advice was always in the back of her mind. But how could she be on guard against the unexpected? And how could she tolerate the thought that there was someone who actually wanted to hurt her? By late afternoon, she had reached the point where she jumped every time anyone spoke to her.

She could attribute two of the accidents to herself, she decided. If she hadn't lost her concentration, she wouldn't have fallen down the stairs; and if she hadn't been driving so fast, she would have seen the debris. That left the ladder and the face powder. Wood rotted, it was as simple as that. And as for the powder, they would have to wait for the chemical analysis to determine what had gone wrong with it.

She loved Jean-Paul, but she wished with all her heart he hadn't come. She wanted these last hours with Richard to be spent happily, not in anger.

By the end of the afternoon, when Clay called, "That's all until tonight," Liana was more than ready to stop. She was tired, irritated, jittery, and unable to endure one more trauma, whether it be a touch or a loud voice.

She ducked behind the changing screen and quickly put on flats, taupe slacks, and a bright red cotton, short-sleeved sweater. The rain had slackened to a fine mist, and she had every intention of taking a walk. But when she emerged, Richard was waiting for her, and one look told her he was still as angry as he had been that morning.

His eyes glinted like ice crystals. "I really didn't expect to see you here."

His sarcasm had the same effect on her as the sound of nails on a chalkboard. "Where did you think I'd be?"

"With Savion, of course. After all, the two of you have been apart almost two weeks. I supposed he would want some *private* time with you. At the very least, I thought he would be here."

"Well, you were wrong on both counts, weren't you? Does that tell you anything?"

"What should it tell me?"

"Oh, I don't know. How about that your suspicions regarding Jean-Paul and me are wrong, in fact, have *always* been wrong?"

"Who has suspicions?" he asked harshly. "I have hard, cold knowledge, sweetheart. Remember? I was there when you went from my bed to his in one very short afternoon."

"I did no such thing!"

He stepped closer, invading and taking control of the air she was trying to pull into her lungs.

"Are you denying that you lived with Savion?"

In her peripheral vision she caught a glimpse of Sara and Clay, unabashedly eaves-dropping, but she was too upset for their presence to matter. "Yes, Richard, I did live with him. He took me in when I had no other place to go."

"Excuse me? What was wrong with where you'd been staying?"

"*You* were there. And I've already told you why I had to leave."

"Yeah. Right. Because you had fallen in love with me. I almost have that part straight. What still bothers me—only a little, you understand—is *why*, loving me as you say you did, you became Savion's lover."

"Dammit, I was *never* Jean-Paul's lover! I've told you that time and again."

"Then, dammit, why can't I believe you?"

"Because you're a fool!"

He raised his hand, and she instinctively recoiled, unsure whether he meant to strike her or caress her. Either act at this moment would have been intolerable to her. Suddenly he turned and walked swiftly from the conservatory.

The overwhelming need to escape seized her— she wanted to go somewhere, *anywhere* that was quiet, isolated, peaceful. She wheeled and ran out the back door of the conservatory.

It was growing darker, but she struck out across the grounds.

Damn Richard! One way or the other he had dominated her entire adult life. It had to stop. The deceit of her father had altered and affected both of their lives. But Richard knew everything now. Why couldn't he understand her side, see more clearly? *Why couldn't he love her?*

She had admitted her foolishness and her stupidity. Their only chance lay in his ability and willingness to let go of the past, but he refused. He seemed blocked about Jean-Paul.

The mist should have cooled her anger. The fast pace she walked should have relieved some of her tension. But she found herself growing more and more agitated. In her mind, *he* was the one who was now being foolish and stupid.

Some time later, she came to a stop in front of Leonora Deverell's crypt and blinked. What on earth was she doing here? Through the increasing darkness, she stared at the letters that spelled Leonora's name. Strangely, her mind went back in years and distance to Paris and another Leonora she had met about a year after she had left Richard. When she had told him that the Leonora she had known there had given up everything for love, he had said he didn't believe in love.

Still, he had shown concern for her safety last night. And today he had been *jealous*. Good heavens! Why hadn't she seen it before? He was wildly jealous of Jean-Paul, even after all these years. He *had* to care!

Hope once more sprang to life within her, but she tried to remain cautious. She had gone through so many highs and lows since she had been here at SwanSea, she wasn't sure how much more she could take.

But Richard had shown tenderness and concern for her. And time and again, he had made love to her as if starving for her. *And* he had displayed unreasonable jealousy. If those weren't the signs of a man in love, what were? Even if he didn't know it.

She had to go to him. Somehow she had to get through his hurt and pride and reach his heart. She would go to him now.

Something sharp struck the back of her head. Leonora's name blurred in front of her eyes, and her knees buckled. She fell to the ground and heard an odd creaking sound of rusty hinges. Fighting against the darkness that threatened to suck her down into it, she tried to make sense of what was happening. But steel-muscled arms gripped her around the waist and dragged her across wet grass, up steps, into a building, finally leaning her against a concrete wall.

Even as she heard the creaking sound again, she struggled to get up. But dizziness overcame her, and she lost her footing. Once more she was falling, and she couldn't stop. She tumbled down a short series of steps, halting only when she struck the side of her head against the hard floor.

Unconsciousness claimed her.

And she didn't hear the scraping of the heavy concrete urn as it was rolled in front of the crypt's doors, sealing her in.

Ten

Clay smiled, feeling a huge sense of relief as he turned away from the crypt and started back to the hotel. At last, something he had done had worked. And in the end, it had been luck rather than elaborate planning that had helped him achieve the goal of putting Liana out of commission long enough to have Sara replace her as the model on this shoot.

Knowing that his time was running out, he'd been racking his brain, trying to decide what he could do next. Jean-Paul's arrival had had him convinced he should abandon his plans. Then two things happened. During his quick visit with Savion this morning, he had seen that the great man wasn't as well as he would like everyone to believe. Then Liana and Zagan had had that argument. Afterwards, Liana had been so upset, she hadn't even noticed him following her. And luck had again been with him when she had gone to the cemetery, and he had happened to notice that with very little effort he could break the crypt's rusty lock.

He hadn't really hurt her, of course. She was only stunned. She would spend an uncomfortable night, but that couldn't be helped. By morning, if she hadn't been found, he would "discover" her. She would be fine, just fine.

Naturally it would have been better if one of the other little accidents he had planned for her had been successful. If she had broken an arm when she had fallen down the stairs, for instance, or if she had used the face powder and developed a rash, he would have had more of an opportunity to photograph Sara.

Yet the ball was the culmination of SwanSea's grand opening and that would work to his advantage. Once the shots he planned to take tonight were seen, he would be able to persuade the publications involved to use a greater number of them than those previously taken. He could even help matters along by exposing several rolls of film, thereby losing quite a few of Liana's shots.

Yes, that's what he would do.

Richard pulled the phone away from his ear and glared at it. Liana still wasn't answering in her room. Either she hadn't returned, or she was ignoring the messages he was leaving with the hotel operator. He slammed the phone back into its cradle.

He supposed he couldn't blame her if she was ignoring his messages. He had hurt her and made her angry, then stormed out of the conservatory.

But that had been a little after six, and it was now nine-thirty. *Where was she?*

He shouldn't have argued with her, he reflected grimly, but just the thought of her and Savion made him deaf, dumb, and blind.

He raked his fingers through his hair, disgusted with himself. A new idea had been steadily growing in him, the idea that he was dead wrong—about Liana and Savion being lovers, about allowing the bitterness of the past eleven years to interfere with the present and the future, and most importantly, about there not being any such thing as love.

Dammit, he'd give her ten more minutes, then he was going to go looking for her.

The pain . . . Liana moaned. her head throbbed; why didn't it stop? Slowly and with great difficulty, she lifted her hand to her forehead and touched something sticky.

She was lying on concrete, she realized, then shivered. Lord, she was cold. She needed to get off the floor. If only her head didn't hurt so much.

Time seemed to pass—she had no idea how much. But she was still on the floor, she noticed. She rolled over and bumped against something concrete . . . a wall? No, because she could feel a corner biting into her shoulder. She levered herself into a sitting position and skimmed her hand upward, over concrete, then to wood. Wood? Her fingers found the upper edge of what seemed to be a large wooden box and curled over the top. Taking a grip, she tried to pull herself up. But the wood broke off and fell to the floor with a crash. She flinched at the loud noise and slumped back down, the dizziness and pain almost overwhelming.

Where was she?

Then she remembered. The sharp pain at the back of her head, Leonora's name blurring in front of her eyes, someone dragging her into a building. *She was in Leonora's crypt!* And she was leaning against the concrete slab on which Leonora's coffin rested!

A sob escaped her, but she quickly clamped her hand over her mouth to stifle it. Was the person who did this to her in here with her? Her heart slammed against her ribs at the thought, and a new kind of chill gripped her—the chill of terror.

But she refused to give into the fear. She searched the darkness of the small burial house until she was assured that she was alone. Good. What now? Think, Liana. Think.

It wasn't pitch black, she realized. In fact, she could see a pale sliver of moonlight. The mist must have cleared. The doors! They must be ajar!

It took her several tries before she was able to stand. She stumbled on the stairs, but finally made it to the source of the light.

She pushed against the doors; they didn't budge. Frantically, she pushed harder. Nothing. Something was blocking the doors.

Tears filled her eyes and she slid down the door to the floor. She was entombed with Leonora Deverell.

Propped against a pile of pillows, Jean-Paul glanced at his watch. Dammit, it was after ten. Why hadn't Liana called him? He had left message after message for her, yet he hadn't heard from her. He knew for a fact the work had been over for hours.

There was only one answer: she had to be with Zagan.

With a muffled curse, he reached for a cheroot and lit it.

He had never known what had happened eleven years ago between the two of them. He only knew, no matter what she said, that she hadn't healed from their love affair. Sometimes when she thought he wasn't looking, he would catch a brief glimpse of pain in her eyes. The bastard had better not hurt her again!

Dammit, but this infection made him feel so powerless! He had come here to help her, and look at him! He had been reduced to leaving messages in between his naps. But *what if something had happened to her?*

A knock sounded at the door, and hopeful that it was Liana, he sat up. "Come in."

"Thank you," Richard said, walking in, his tone anything but polite.

Jean-Paul's black eyebrows drew together in a scowl. "What the hell do you want?"

Richard's gaze scanned the room, then came back to rest on Jean-Paul. "I want to know where Liana is."

With an insouciance he hoped would madden Zagan, Jean-Paul settled himself comfortably against the pillows and took a long draw on his cheroot. "Assuming I knew, do you think I would tell you?"

Richard's first impulse was to drag the man from the bed and beat the information out of him. But the other man's obviously weakened condition made that choice impossible; there would be no triumph in winning such a one-sided struggle. Besides, instinct told him winning the mental battle would be the greater victory.

He chose a chair and sat down. "You and Liana are very close, aren't you?"

Jean-Paul bared his teeth in a mockery of a smile. "Very."

"Frankly, I expected to find her here."

"And if you had found her here, what meaning would you have applied to it?"

Richard crossed his legs, resting the ankle of one leg over the knee of the other leg. "That is none of your business."

"Probably not, but I know the answer all the same. Tell me, Zagan, what has Liana told you about us?"

"That you and she have never been lovers."

"Yet I would be willing to wager that you believe we have been and probably still are."

Richard stared impassively at Jean-Paul. He had viewed this man as an adversary for so long that he couldn't bring himself to admit what he was saying had been true up until a short time ago.

Jean-Paul exhaled a long stream of smoke. "I find your attitude truly remarkable. I've known Liana slightly longer than you have, and I've always found that, though she sometimes keeps things to herself, she never lies."

Richard's anger grew—not at Savion, but at the circumstances that had made it possible for this man to know more about Liana than he did. He stood and shoved his hands into his pockets. "Are you going to tell me where she is?"

"Whatever happened between the two of you," Jean-Paul went on in a calm voice as if Richard hadn't spoken, "hurt her badly. When she came to me, she was in pieces. I did the only thing I could do. I gave her work. Night and day, using any excuse I could think of, I photographed her. I wore her out so that she could sleep at night. And when she was awake, I worked her so hard, she sometimes forgot to think of you for minutes at a time. The side benefit was that the haunting, mysterious sadness I captured with those pictures intensified her beauty and catapulted both of us to fame."

"How lucky for you," Richard said woodenly.

"Yes, it was. And for Liana, too. She didn't have you anymore, but she had success. Ironic, isn't it? In some strange way, I might actually owe you a debt of gratitude, which is one of the reasons, Zagan, if I knew where she was, I would tell you. Another reason why I would tell you is that I fear she is in some sort of danger and I don't like the idea of her being out somewhere by herself. It might not be safe, and I'm too damned weak to go looking for her."

A confirmation of his own fears didn't improve Richard's mood. "There's no need for you to look. Now that I know she's not here, I'll find her."

Jean-Paul waited until Richard had almost reached the door before he spoke again. "I put her back together once, Zagan. I don't want to have to do it again."

Richard quietly shut the door after himself.

The orchestra swung into the upbeat Gershwin tune, "I've Got Rhythm," and some of the richest, most influential people in America began to dance.

Clay viewed Sara through the lens of his camera and felt a special thrill of satisfaction. Sara had never understood why he loved to photograph her. But he had seen something in her no one else had. An intriguing woman lay beneath the shy child, and in his camera lens, her fresh loveliness would be illuminated for all the world to see.

The magnificent gold and silver ballroom was beginning to fill. At his instructions, Sara was posed against a pillar, wearing a black velvet gown that might have been fitted on Liana, but looked as if it had been made for Sara. She didn't seem happy, he noted, but once they got started, he would be able to cajole her into the right mood.

He planned to capture her in her stillness and black gown and frame her with the ball's color and movement.

She was going to do for his career what Liana had done for Jean-Paul's.

"Clay, do you know where Liana is?"

Richard Zagan's voice held a dangerous edge, cutting in on Clay's euphoric mood. A wary glance over his shoulder told him the man was in a black mood. "As it happens, I don't. Now if you would excuse us, we've got work to do."

Richard took Clay by the shoulders and forcibly turned him around. "I'll excuse you after I've gotten the answers I want. Isn't Liana supposed to be modeling tonight?"

"Yes, but as you can see, she didn't show up, so we're having to start without her."

Richard glanced at Sara. She looked pretty, he thought, but not as lovely as Liana would in the same dress. He returned his gaze to Clay. "Have you tried to find Liana?"

Clay felt one corner of his mouth twitch and tried to relax. Nothing could go wrong now. Not when he was so close to achieving his goal. "I don't understand why you're upset. It's obvious what's happened. After your argument with her in the conservatory earlier, she packed up and left."

"She wouldn't have left, knowing how important these last shots were, at least not without telling someone," Sara said, speaking up unexpectedly. "She's too professional."

"I agree," Richard said, "and I repeat my question."

Clay could feel his control slipping and drew a deep breath. "The answer is yes. Steve and Rosalyn insisted on going to look for her. I told them there was nothing to worry about and that I needed them, but—oh, good, there they are now. Steve, I need you to adjust that light—"

"Did you find her?" Richard asked Steve.

The younger man shook his head. "We even had a bellhop let us into her room."

"Her clothes are still there," Rosalyn said, "but there was no sign of her."

Clay wanted to scream. *Why didn't these people just let it go, for God's sake!* Didn't they understand the importance of what he was doing? "Liana will show up when she's ready to."

Richard turned on him. "You just said she'd packed up and left."

Clay threw up his arms. "How do I know where she is? All I know is I've got to get this shoot underway. And if she's not professional enough to show up, there are others who can replace her."

Richard had never liked Clay, and if he hadn't felt every moment was important, he would have decked him. He started to leave, but felt something stopping him. He turned back to Clay. "There's just one more thing. Have you gotten back the analysis of the face powder?"

"Not yet. I probably should follow up to make sure my friend received it. The mail is so unreliable." He turned to Sara and Steve. "In the meantime, people, we've got to get underway."

Ignoring Clay, Steve gazed at Richard. "I'll help you look for her."

"I will too," Sara said.

Richard shook his head. "Thanks, but I'll find her."

Wind whistled through the iron structure of the gazebo, emphasizing its emptiness. Richard slammed his hand against a wrought iron support. Dammit! Where was Liana?

Anxiously, he stared out at the night. Fortunately, the sky had cleared and he wasn't having trouble seeing, but the air was cool, and the grass had been damp beneath his feet as he had walked. Was she cold, he wondered. Was she hurt?

His mind refused to take that next awful step of imagination and wonder if she were dead. She *had* to be all right.

Lord, Liana, where are you?

Outside of her hotel room, they had been so few places together. Where would she go? Or, God forbid, where would someone take her? His jaw tightened at the thought. Confidence aside, he would give himself only a short time to find her, and then he would contact the police.

He could hear the music being played in the ballroom. "Embraceable You." He had never noticed before, but it was really a lovely song. If Liana were here, he thought, he would take her in his arms and dance with her. They had never danced, but he knew she would be light, graceful, exquisite to hold. They would dance as long as they both wanted. Then they would make love.

The afternoon he had found her here, he had taken her down to the cushioned bench, kissed her, touched her. That had been his first indication of how much he had still loved her, only he had been too blind to see it then and too proud to admit that love even if he had seen it.

Liana had been right this afternoon. He *was* a fool. If he had acknowledged even a particle of his love, he might have her with him now.

He remembered the puzzled looks Rosalyn and Steve had given him at the confident way he had said he would find Liana. They might wonder where his certainty came from, he thought grimly, but he knew he had no alternative. He *had* to find Liana. He couldn't live the rest of his life without her.

Chilled to the bone, her head dully aching, Liana sat on the inner steps of the crypt. She hugged herself for comfort and warmth, unable to remember how it felt not to be cold or have her head hurt.

She also didn't know how long she had been staring at the long, boxy shape of Leonora's coffin just a short distance away.

From the first, she'd been affected by the tragic story of the young Leonora. Her interest hadn't made sense then, nor did it now, but her heart still went out to the woman. Her happiness had been cut so short, and now there was no one left alive who mourned her. Except her, Liana thought. And now she was sharing her burial place.

She touched the dried blood caked at her temple. During the long hours she had been there, she had fought against the pain and the cold, but most of all she had fought against the fear. She supposed under the circumstances it would be natural for her to believe that she was fated to die here. Actually, though, this experience had made Liana want happiness all the more.

The Leonora she had known in Paris had told her that one day she would find true love. Well, she had already found it. She had been foolish enough to let go of that love once, but never again.

She refused to die there. She had too much living to do yet, too much loving. She formed an image in her mind of Richard and concentrated on it with everything that was in her. He was her heart, her life. He would come for her.

A long time later, she heard movement outside.

Just for a moment, she had to fight back the terror that the person who had put her in there had come back. But almost as soon as the terror came, it vanished. Somehow she knew it was Richard.

"Liana? Are you in there?"

She scrambled to her feet, almost losing her balance again in her eagerness to get to the doors. "Richard?"

"Liana? Dear God, you *are* in there! Are you all right?"

"Yes, yes, I'm fine."

"Hang on, honey, I'll have you out in just a minute."

There was the sound of the concrete urn being pulled away, then the doors were opened, and Richard stepped inside and swept her into his arms. He crushed her to him, trembling with relief and happiness that he was finally holding her again.

Her skin felt cold, but she was alive and breathing. He felt as if he had just been delivered from a lifetime sentence in hell. He buried his face in her hair and breathed in her scent. He didn't want to let her go, not now, not ever, but finally, supporting her with his hands on her arms, he pulled back and looked down at her. "Are you really all right?"

"I think so," she said, unable to prevent her voice from shaking.

"What happened? Who put you in here?"

"I don't know who. They stunned me by hitting me in the back of the head, then they dragged me in here. I guess water from the rain we had earlier had seeped beneath the doors. When I tried to get up, I slipped down the stairs and hit my head on the floor. I'm not sure how long I was out. What time is it?"

He glanced at the luminescent dial of his watch. "One-thirty in the morning. Lord, Liana, you've been trapped in the crypt all this time?" At her nod, he swung her up into his arms and held her close. "Let's get out of here."

"I can't think of anything I'd like more," she murmured. But as he turned with her, she glanced over his shoulder, unable to resist the compulsion to have one more look at the eternal resting place of Leonora Deverell, the place that could so easily have become her own tomb.

Moonlight illuminated the inside of the crypt with an eerie silver light, enabling her to see that the entire end panel of the coffin had fallen to the ground and opened the interior of the coffin to view.

Her breath caught in her throat.

Richard carried Liana clutched closely to his heart and entered SwanSea by the front doors. Because the ball was still going on, he wasn't surprised to see that the entry hall was empty except for a small staff at the desk tucked discreetly off to the side. But he was surprised to see Jean-Paul and Clay come into the hall through a side door, talking heatedly.

"Dammit," Clay was saying, "you gave this assignment to me, now let me do it."

Pale, but determined, Jean-Paul towered over Clay. "As soon as you answer some of my questions."

"I don't have time for this. Sara, Rosalyn, and Steve are back in the ballroom waiting for me."

"And where is Liana?"

"How the hell should I know?"

Richard glanced down at Liana. Her eyes were closed, her dark lashes lay against the almost colorless skin of her cheeks. When he found the person who had done this to her . . . He looked back at the two men. "Here she is." Clay and Jean-Paul both jerked around toward them. Jean-Paul's expression was of utter relief. Clay's expression, very briefly, was of anger.

Jean-Paul rushed toward them. "Mon Dieu, you have found her! Liana, what happened to you? Are you all right?"

She opened her eyes. "You look awful, Jean-Paul. You should be in bed."

"Bah! I have been there all day. I couldn't stand the wait one more moment, so I came down to see what I could do."

Richard's mouth quirked with faint amusement. "You didn't trust me to tell you I had found her, did you?" he asked, still keeping an eye on Clay who had slowly crossed the distance to them.

Jean-Paul's dark brows rose. "And would you have told me?"

"Eventually." Richard smiled briefly before turning his attention to Clay. "How is your shoot going?"

"Fine." Clay cast a disgruntled glance at Jean-Paul. "Or at least it was."

"You knew, didn't you?" Richard's suddenly quiet voice carried such murderous intent, each word was like a knife thrown.

Jean-Paul stilled.

"Knew what?" Clay asked warily.

"Knew where Liana was—because you put her there, didn't you?"

Liana stiffened, and he tightened his arms around her, trying to reassure her. "I'll take you to your room in just a minute," he whispered.

"I had my suspicions," Jean-Paul said, his expression stricken, "but I didn't want to accuse without proof."

"I'm sure you also didn't want to believe that your protégé could do something like this."

"Why?" Liana whispered. "Why, Clay?"

"I didn't want to hurt you," Clay said, his words coming out in a rush, "but I needed for Sara to be the model here. No matter how brilliant my pictures of you would be, Liana, I could never gain fame by photographing you. You would photograph beautifully in the dark, and everyone in the business knows it. But Sara was an unknown—"

"Did she know what you were doing?" Jean-Paul asked, interrupting, plainly over feeling bad that Clay could have done such a thing. He was angry now, and it showed in the coldness of his black eyes.

"No. She's always been reluctant to let me take pictures of her, but I knew she couldn't refuse if I put her in the position of saving the assignment."

"Did you rig the light to fall?"

"Yes, yes," he said, his impatient tone implying they were asking all the wrong questions. What was important here was his work. "And I added a caustic ingredient to the powder. I just wanted you out of commission for the rest of the shoot, Liana. I didn't want to seriously hurt you."

Richard was having a hard time keeping the rage he felt under control, and because he was, he spoke softly. "What about the nails and boards on the road?"

"No. The only other thing I did was tamper with the ladder. I had the second ladder so that Sara would be sure to take the one whose rung I had broken. You couldn't even tell that I had broken the rung, then glued it back together, could you?" His eyes shone with excitement as he turned back to Jean-Paul. "I want you to see the work I've done tonight, Jean-Paul. I think you'll agree it's extraordinary. I knew that out of everyone, you would be the one to understand. Nothing is more important to you than your work."

"You *damned* fool."

Liana shut her eyes and turned her face into Richard's chest. He was torn. He wanted to rip Clay limb from limb, but Liana was his first consideration. She had been through more than enough already.

"I'll take care of it," Jean-Paul said.

Even though it seemed Jean-Paul sensed some of what he was feeling, Richard's old prejudices automatically reared, making him hesitate. But the woman in his arms and the love he had for her forced him to look at Savion without the blinders of his jealousy, and what he saw reassured him. Savion had a toughness, a fortitude, and a gritty type of integrity that transcended the physical strain he was under. Richard finally nodded, accepting that Savion would do whatever was necessary. He loved Liana, too.

But she was going to be *his* wife.

He carried her to the elevator.

Eleven

Liana awoke to a sun-filled room, the softness of the four poster bed, and Richard, lying beside her, gazing at her.

With a gentle smile, she reached out to stroke the stubble of his morning beard. "How long have you been watching me?"

"Most of the night. I didn't want anything more to happen to you." He took her fingers and kissed each tip. "When I think of what you must have gone through . . ."

"It's over, Richard. Besides, I knew you would find me."

He smiled. "Did you? I don't know where your confidence came from, but somehow I felt I would find you, too. I *had* to find you."

Her face shadowed. "Clay . . ."

"I've already spoken with Savion this morning. Clay was taken away last night. What happens to him will depend on the courts and maybe even the doctors. But like you said, it's over. It's time for us to go on."

She searched his eyes, saw the warmth and

tenderness, and remembered the hope she had felt yesterday evening before Clay had closed her in the crypt. "There are some things I'd like to say to you."

"No, let me go first. Looking back on that day in Paris when you left, I realize now I should have gone after you. I don't usually let anything get in the way of what I want. But with you, I couldn't think rationally. If I had, I would have realized that what we had together those two weeks was the real thing and you had to have had another reason. But instead of trying to find out that reason, or even trying to change your mind, I set my pride and ego above my happiness and fooled myself into believing I would be fine without you. But Lord was I wrong! I loved you then, Liana, and I love you now." His voice broke. "With all my heart, with all my soul."

She had had hope, but hearing the actualization of her dream stunned her. "You do?"

"If you weren't hurt, I would show you how much."

"I'm fine," she whispered, sliding her arms around his neck. "Show me."

Regretfully, he shook his head. "You've been hurt."

"Your love is the best medicine I could possibly have."

He groaned. For her sake, he shouldn't let her seduce him like this, but he was helpless in the face of his love and his need for her. After the terror and uncertainty of last night, when he hadn't known where she was or in what condition he would find her, he *needed* to make love to her. It would be a celebration of life and of their future. But . . .

"I love you, Richard," she murmured, unknowingly ending his hesitation.

He kissed her gently, touched her softly. He gathered up all the tenderness, love, and passion of which he was capable and poured it over her. He felt her tremble and trembled with her. When her skin heated, his did too. When she moaned, he followed with one of his own.

They were together in every possible way. Nothing was forced; everything came naturally. Each moment that passed was treated as precious, each word that was spoken was valued. Like a flower receiving its first spring rain, she soaked up everything he gave her, then blossomed and returned it to him tenfold.

Liana was gone. Richard knew it even before he came completely awake. Panicked, he sat straight up in bed and shot a look around the room. Empty! She couldn't have left him, not now, now when it seemed they had found happiness. He glanced at the clock. He had only been asleep an hour. What could have happened?

He was standing, zipping up his pants, when she walked out of the bathroom, dressed. The relief he felt was so profound he almost collapsed back onto the bed.

"What's wrong?" she asked, instantly concerned because of the odd expression on his face.

He went to her and took her into his arms. "You're going to have to be patient with me. I'm paranoid where you're concerned. We've been through so much. . . ."

"I understand," she said quietly. "I have the same fears. But we shouldn't allow ourselves to worry anymore. We're not going to lose what we have ever again."

For her and with effort, he grinned. "I'll work on taking you for granted."

With a laugh, she stood on her tiptoes and kissed him. "Let's not go quite that far."

"It looks like you're going somewhere. Why didn't you wake me?"

"I didn't want to bother you. Besides, I wasn't planning to be gone that long."

"Where *are* you going?" he asked, reaching for a shirt.

Her brow knitted, not at his question, but at an inner thought. "I need to speak to Caitlin. Something's bothering me, and I'm hoping she can help clear it up."

"Well, wherever you're going, I'm going with you. From now on, that's the rule. We've been apart too long. If you want to go on an out-of-town assignment, I'll go with you. If I have to go out of town on business, you'll go with me. We're never going to be apart again."

His vehemence surprised her and her heart threatened to overflow with happiness. "I'm going to like that rule."

They left the room, hand in hand, and walked down the hall to the elevator. When it glided to a smooth stop on the fourth floor and the doors opened, Caitlin was waiting for them.

She anxiously scanned Liana. "You've had the worst time here, and I feel just awful about it."

Liana laughed lightly. It felt good to laugh so easily and so often. "Don't give it another thought. It wasn't your fault." She glanced at Richard. "Besides, when I look back on my stay here, I guarantee I will remember only the good things that have come out of it."

Caitlin's gaze darted back and forth between Liana and Richard, noting their joined hands, and placing the obvious interpretation on the situation. She slowly smiled. "In that case, I feel better. Now, what was it you wanted to ask me?"

"It's about Leonora Deverell, the first mistress of SwanSea."

"Yes. What about her?"

"Is there a portrait of her somewhere?"

"As a matter of fact, I've only recently had her portrait brought down from the attic and cleaned. I had it hung in my suite. Would you like to see it?"

"Very much."

Liana glanced at Richard. He looked distinctly puzzled, and she squeezed his hand. "I don't want to say anything until I'm sure." The returning squeeze of his hand told her he accepted her wish not to explain further right now. It might have been only a small sign of trust to some, but she knew it was a forerunner of all the faith and confidence that would grow between them in the coming years.

Caitlin led them to a set of double doors at the end of the hall to a suite decorated, like the rest of the hotel, completely in the art nouveau period.

Over the mantel hung a portrait of a young woman with lovely, aristocratic features, wearing a blue dress that frothed around her ankles like a summer cloud. Her soft eyes held a tinge of sadness, but her smile was sweet and hopeful.

Liana smiled back in recognition.

Though many years had passed from the time the portrait had been painted until the time Liana had known her, the woman's sweet smile, her soft eyes, and most of all the aristocratic bone structure of her face had remained the same. "Leonora," she whispered.

Misunderstanding, Caitlin nodded. "That's right."

"Liana," Richard said slowly, his eyes narrowing on the sight of the exquisite lily pinned at the young woman's breast, "that's your brooch."

"Your brooch?" Caitlin said, startled. "You mean *this* is where I'd seen it? But that couldn't be. All of the jewelry has stayed in the family. We haven't sold or given any away. How would you have gotten Leonora's brooch?"

"She gave it to me."

"That's impossible. She died in 1898."

"I knew her, Caitlin."

"You mean this Leonora is the same Leonora who was your neighbor in Paris?" Richard asked. "The old lady who gave you the brooch?"

"That's right. Maybe we'd better sit down while I explain."

She settled onto the settee and waited while Richard came down beside her and Caitlin chose a chair. Then she began.

"Leonora Redmond was one-hundred-and-one years old when I moved in next door to her. She was bedridden, but very alert, and we grew close. She told me that at seventeen she had married an older man because it was expected of her by her family. She had done her duty and tried hard with the marriage, but love between them never grew. Only his business and the great house he had built were important to him.

"One summer, four years after her wedding, her husband hired a young painter to come to the house and paint her portrait. His name was Wyatt Redmond. They fell in love, but Leonora viewed their affair as hopeless and sent the young man away. He left around midsummer and went home to Paris. But once there he quickly came to understand that he would never be able to live without her and booked the first passage back. He told Edward he had returned to finish the portrait, but his real intent was to convince Leonora to leave her husband and run away with him. He had also brought with him a present for her—the lily he had bought in Paris from the workshop of René Lalique. It was the only piece of jewelry she took with her when she left."

Caitlin had been listening closely. "But I still don't understand. If she fled to Paris with her lover, who is buried in her crypt?"

"No one. I was there, last night, remember?" The thought made her reach over and take Richard's hand again. Before this morning, she hadn't known how comforting it was to hold the hand of the man you loved. "When I awoke on the floor, I tried to hold onto the coffin to help myself up—although at the time I didn't know what it was. But the wood must have been so rotten, it gave way, and I heard it crumble to the floor. When Richard opened the doors, the moonlight streamed in, and I was able to see that the coffin is empty." She paused. "I thought it was love that had made Edward set Leonora's crypt apart from the others. Now I understand. It was bitterness."

"But why would any man go through a mock funeral for his wife," Richard asked, "knowing full well she was still alive?"

"I can answer that part," Caitlin said. "Because of pride. What I know of Edward came from listening to my grandfather, Jake, talk of him. I learned that Edward was a hard, driven man of enormous pride. I'm sure it never occurred to him that Leonora would leave him, and when she did, he would have been quite disconcerted and mortified. His number one priority would have been not to get her back, but to hide the fact from society that his wife had left him for another man."

"Pride," Richard murmured softly. It seemed he and Edward Deverell had something in common.

"And I know for a fact," Caitlin said, continuing, "that Edward wouldn't have let her take John."

"Who was John?" Richard and Liana asked simultaneously.

"Their only child."

Liana slowly nodded. "That must have been her regret. She never spoke of her child to me, but she did tell me that when her husband died in 1929, she and Wyatt married. Wyatt achieved only a modest success with his painting, but according to Leonora, they lived very happily until his death in the early nineteen-seventies."

"This is a remarkable story, Liana," Caitlin said, shaking her head in amazement. "I can't wait to tell my family. I've learned the most interesting things about my ancestors since I've inherited SwanSea."

"It seems both Edward and Leonora chose to live with deceit all their lives," Liana said thoughtfully, still caught up in the story. Suddenly she turned to Richard and a look of understanding passed between them. They had been through their own years of deceit, but they had been lucky enough to come out on the other side of those years with love.

"In the end, Edward died a lonely man," Caitlin said.

"And Leonora obviously found a peace of sorts and a happiness," Liana said. "But poor John never really knew his mother. To leave your child has to be the hardest decision any woman has to make. Leonora must have been desperate. She must have felt as if she would shrivel up and die if she stayed here at SwanSea."

Caitlin nodded. "Knowing what I know of the hard man Edward was, I would agree with you. At least she would have had the comfort of knowing that Edward would give his son everything she couldn't. It's not a decision you or I would make, but then I don't feel I should judge Leonora. Only she knew what her life was like."

Liana glanced at Richard, and they both came to their feet. "I feel like going for a walk in the sunshine, maybe out to the gazebo. Caitlin, do you think we could have our breakfast served at the gazebo?"

The current mistress of SwanSea smiled. "Well, I seem to recall telling you to ask for anything that you wanted. I'm sure we can manage it. Just tell me that you will come back to SwanSea one day soon."

"You can count on it," Richard said.

Halfway between the great house of SwanSea and the gazebo, Liana and Richard stopped and turned to each other. The day was clear, the light almost incandescent. The sun bathed the two of them and all of SwanSea in its warmth, making it hard for them to believe there had ever been shadows.

Richard's gaze was adoring and cherishing. "When I think of how easily our lives could have been destroyed by pride and deceit . . ."

"I know, but it didn't happen. We both came here, scarred and in pain, but we'll be leaving together. We have our love back, and it's deeper and all the stronger for what we've been through."

"Thank God."

A tremor shuddered through him that she felt in her own body.

"I'll never have to spend another lonely night," he said. "You'll be there—your soft voice, your incredible beauty, you."

She smiled, a different smile, a special smile. "There might be a baby there with us, too, one conceived here at SwanSea. Have you thought of that?"

He chuckled. "Thought of it, hoped for it, prayed for it. But if it doesn't happen now or in the future, my life will still be complete. If children come, I will feel that much more blessed, but you are all I'll ever want or need."

The timeless rhythm of the sea surged behind them. She had come to love the sound and this place. But there was also another place. "Can we fly to France? I want to show you my little house."

"We'll spend our honeymoon there, and in the years ahead, if children come, we'll take them there."

"I love you," she whispered to him.

"I love you," he whispered back to her.

At the gazebo, the wind wound in and out of the decorative ironwork, smoothing across the green and blue cushions, picking up a single feather of a tiny sea bird and sweeping it down the steps.

Today, if there were tears heard here, they would be tears of happiness. And there would also be laughter. Most of all, though, there would be love.

THE EDITOR'S CORNER

It's been a while since we acknowledged and thanked the many people here at Bantam who work so hard to make our LOVESWEPTs the best they can be. Aside from our small editorial staff, members of the art department, managing editorial department, production, sales, and marketing departments, to name a few, all contribute their expertise to the project. The department whose input is most apparent to you, the reader, is that of our art department, so I'd like to mention them briefly this month.

Getting the cover art exactly right isn't an easy task. No two people ever envision the characers the same way—and think of how many people read our books! Our art director, Beverly Leung, knows how important it is for you to have a beautiful cover to look at. Her job starts by commissioning an artist for a particular book. The artist is given a description sheet prepared by the author herself. After models who most closely resemble the characters are selected, a photographic shoot is done, and from those photos the artist/illustrator creates first a sketch and finally a painting for the cover.

During the entire process Beverly works to ensure we—and ultimately you—are pleased with the finished artwork. She's done a fabulous job since taking on the assignment, and it's reflected in the gorgeous covers we're able to bring you. Thanks, Beverly.

Now on to the good stuff! Next month's LOVESWEPTs feature heroes so yummy, anyone on a diet should beware!

Kay Hooper weaves another magical web around you with **THROUGH THE LOOKING GLASS**, LOVESWEPT #408, the next in her *Once Upon a Time . . .* series. Financial wizard Gideon Hughes fully intends to shut down the carnival he had inherited. But when he arrives to check it out, he's instantly enchanted by manager Maggie Durant—and balance sheets loose all interest for him. Gideon is intrigued and unnerved by Maggie's forthrightness, but something compels him to explore the deep and strange feelings she stirs in him. Then Maggie openly declares her love for Gideon and in so doing, lays claim to his heart. Amid clowns, gypsies, and magicians, Gideon and the silver-haired siren find the most wondrous love—and together they create their own Wonderland.

In **PRIVATE EYES**, LOVESWEPT #409, Charlotte Hughes delivers the kind of story you ask for most often—one that combines lighthearted humor with powerful emotion. Private investigator Jack Sloan resents being asked to train his

(continued)

partner's niece, Ashley Rogers. He takes one look at her and decides she doesn't belong on an undercover assignment, she belongs in a man's arms—preferably in his. But he soon discovers he's underestimated the lovely single mother of two. Ashley works harder than he ever imagined, and her desire to win his approval tugs at his heart—a heart he thought had long ago gone numb. Charlotte puts these two engaging characters in some hilarious situations—and also in some intimate ones. Don't miss this very entertaining romance!

Sandra Chastain often focuses on people living in small towns, and her knack for capturing the essence of a community and the importance of belonging really makes her books special. In **RUN WILD WITH ME**, LOVESWEPT #410, Sandra brings together a wicked-looking cowboy, and a feisty lady law officer. Andrea Fleming has spent her life in Arcadia, Georgia, and she's convinced it's where she belongs. Her one attempt to break away had ended in heartache and disaster. Sam Farley is a stranger in a town that doesn't take kindly to outsiders. He doesn't understand how someone can have ties to a place—until he falls for Andrea. She makes the handsome wanderer crave what he's never known. This is a touching, emotional love story of two lost people who find their true soul mates.

Deborah Smith's heroes are never lacking in good looks or virility—and the hero of **HONEY AND SMOKE**, LOVESWEPT #411, is no exception. Ex-marine Max Templeton could have walked off the cover of *Soldier of Fortune* magazine. But when he encounters Betty Quint in a dark mountain cave, he finds in her one worthy adversary. Betty is a city girl who has moved back to the town of her ancestors to return to the basics and run a small catering business and restaurant. She can't believe the man beneath the camouflage and khaki is also the local justice of the peace! Of course, there's no peace for her once Max invades her life. But Betty is looking for commitment. She has dreams of marriage and family, and Max runs his wedding chapel as if it's all in fun—and with the knowledge that marriage is definitely not for him. You'll love being along for the ride as Betty convinces Max to believe in a perfect future, and Max proves to Betty that Rambo has a heart!

Doris Parmett has a lot of fun inventing her wonderful heroes and heroines and researching her stories. For her latest book she visited a local cable television station and had a great time. She was asked to appear on a talk show,

(continued)

and it went so well, they invited her back. Absorbing as much atmosphere and information as she could, Doris returned to work and created the love story we'll bring you next month. In **OFF LIMITS**, LOVESWEPT #412, Joe Michaels and Liz Davis make television screens melt with their weekly hit show. But off camera, Liz fights to keep things all business. Joe refuses to deny the sexual tension that sizzles between them and vows to prove to the vulnerable woman behind the glamorous image that a man can be trusted, that their life together would be no soap opera. These two characters produce a whirlwind of passionate emotion that sweeps the reader along!

What woman hasn't fantasized about being pursued by a ruggedly gorgeous man? Well, in **BLUE DALTON**, LOVESWEPT #413 by Glenna McReynolds, our heroine, Blue, finds the experience exhausting when tracker Walker Evans stalks her into the Rockies. Blue is after the treasure she believes her father left to her alone, and Walker thinks his is the valid claim. When Walker captures her, she can't help but succumb to wild sensation and has no choice but to share the search. Confused by the strength of her desire for Walker, she tries to outsmart him—but her plan backfires along with her vow not to love him. Only Glenna can blend exciting elements of adventure so successfully with the poignant and heartfelt elements that make a story a true romance. Don't miss this unique book!

We're pleased and proud to feature a devoted LOVESWEPT reader from down under as our Fan of the Month for June. Isn't it wonderful to know stories of love and romance are treasured and enjoyed throughout the world!

Hope your summer is filled with great reading pleasures. Sincerely,

Susann Brailey

Susann Brailey
Editor
LOVESWEPT
Bantam Books
666 Fifth Avenue
New York, NY 10103

FAN OF THE MONTH

Wilma Stubbs

It gives me great pleasure to represent the Australian fans of the LOVESWEPT series, and there are many as evidenced by the fact that one has to be early to get titles by favorite authors such as Kay Hooper, Barbara Boswell, etc.

I have been reading LOVESWEPTs since early 1984 when the Australian publisher distributed a booklet comprised of excerpts from the first titles. I was hooked—and impatient! So I wrote a plaintive letter to New York for a publication date, and the nice people there sent back a letter full of information.

As the mother of two semi-adults with their associated interests and friends, and the wife of a man who has worked shift work for twenty-five years, I've always found romantic fiction to be my favorite retreat. LOVESWEPTs cover a broad range of moods—from the sensuousness of Sandra Brown to the humor of Billie Green to the depth of Mary Kay McComas to the imaginativeness of Iris Johansen, particularly her Clanad series with the delightful touch of mystique.

I have often recommended to troubled friends that they read some of the above authors in order to gain a balance to their lives. It seems to refresh one's spirits to dip into other lives and gain a better perspective on one's own.

THE DELANEY DYNASTY

THE SHAMROCK TRINITY

THE DELANEYS OF KILLAROO

THE DELANEYS: *The Untamed Years*

THE DELANEYS II